A HORSE FOR X.Y.Z.

w/b

Fmoe

A HORSE FOR X. Y. Z.
by Louise Moeri

illustrated by Gail Owens

E. P. DUTTON   NEW YORK

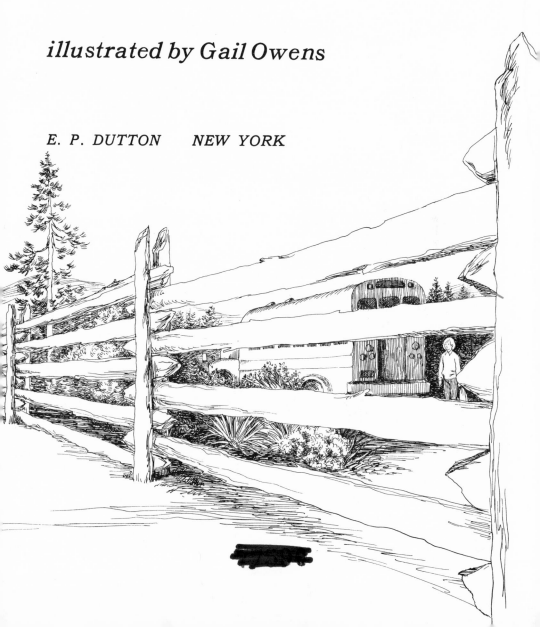

Library of Congress Cataloging in Publication Data

Moeri, Louise   A horse for X. Y. Z.

SUMMARY: When a twelve-year-old girl seizes a chance
to ride a spirited horse, her ride becomes more than
she anticipated.

[1. Horses—Fiction]   I. Owens, Gail.   II. Title.
PZ7.M7214Ho   [Fic]   76–55739   ISBN 0–525–32220–5

Published simultaneously in Canada by Clarke,
Irwin & Company Limited, Toronto and Vancouver

Editor: Ann Durell
Designer: Meri Shardin
Printed in the U.S.A.   First Edition
10 9 8 7 6 5 4 3 2 1

To my daughter, Patricia

1 Riding Arena
2 Stable
3 Corral
4 Tennis Courts and
  Track
5 Bathhouse
6 Pasture
7 Lake
8 Baseball Field
9 Woodshed

10 Cookhouse
11 Dormitory
12 North Dormitory
13 Veranda
14 Loading Zone
15 Shelter
16 Lookout Point
17 Where Solveig camps
   under Rimrock
18 Truck Parked Here

– – – – Fire Flower Trail

•—•—•— Dirt Road into Hills

→ ——→ Unmarked Road taken
         by Solveig as she left
         Shelter

•••••••• Steep Foot Trail down
         Cliff

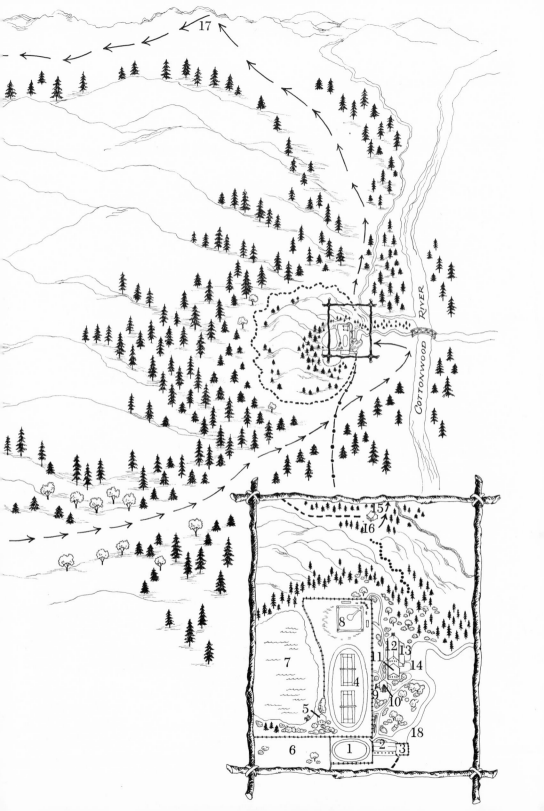

A HORSE FOR X. Y. Z.

Chapter 1

SOLVEIG stared angrily at the back of Miss P's neck. It was red and wrinkled above her crisp white collar, just like her grim old face was red and wrinkled from scowling at millions and millions of girls who just wanted to be girls, for Pete's sake.

The line shuffled toward the bus and Miss P, pencil in hand, crossed a name off her clipboard list as each girl boarded. "Ames, Hester. Berkley, June. Cavanaugh, Roxie. Donaldson, Claire. Evers, Nan—" One for each letter of the alphabet, and always in proper order. Solveig wondered how she always managed that—on every bus Miss P loaded full of girls going to and from anything—play days, concerts, even dental check-ups and chest x rays—Miss P always managed to have a girl for nearly every letter in the alphabet except X, Y, and Z. Suddenly Solveig longed to be named Xenia Yseult Zilch so she could round out the tally and be the last one on the bus (and be photographed waving a dramatic good-bye) instead of being plain Solveig Nilsson thumping along in no particular place in the middle of the alphabet and the middle of the line.

Her small duffel bag banged against her knee as "Nilsson,

Solveig—" rang out and she clambered up the high steps into the bus. "Actually," she muttered, "my name is Xenia Y. Zilch and I'm about to accept a dangerous mission. This bag contains the formula for the ultra-secret pickle-juice bomb, and I'm going to deliver it to—"

The bus was beginning to rock under the stamping of feet as, pressured by Miss P, the girls first in line were settling on the front seats. Most of the comfortable ones were already taken by the time Solveig lumbered down the aisle. So, added to a disappointing week largely devoted to sideline-standing here at Camp Ahwanee was now going to be a slow, torturous ride back to the ivy-covered walls of Coldbrook Academy. Solveig reached the back of the bus—her seat was directly beside the emergency exit—and paused for a last look at the camp.

Outside the bus the late-afternoon sun slanted down over the buildings and playing fields. Autumn leaves and dying grass gave a soft luster to its undistinguished outlines: the weathered, two-story log dormitory with its stone chimneys, a bathhouse near the lake, the cookhouse with an attached woodshed, some equipment sheds, stable and riding arena, and a white-fenced corral. Mountains, thickly forested, surrounded the small valley like a herd of wild beasts who would close in and devour it all the minute they were gone.

In the corral the camp's horses stood in tail-switching pairs, waiting for a man named Kramer, who had a ranch nearby, to come and take them away next morning. The camp was closing after this weekend, as the crisp October days meandered on like a shallow stream, and not a single human soul would be left here after this bus was loaded.

Cars carrying camp personnel were also in the loading zone, their motors running softly. Bored faces at the windows, cleaned at last of their polite smiles, cast some doubt on how much they cared—really cared—about a busload of girls from Coldbrook Academy. Good riddance, the faces seemed to say.

And good riddance to you, thought Solveig. I'll be glad to see the last of you, too. Who needs a whole committee of people saying, "No, you can't do it—you're too young—too small—too inexperienced." Not that she wouldn't have enjoyed the week at the camp if she'd gotten half a chance. Part of the reason she worked so hard to maintain the level of scholarship demanded by Coldbrook was because trips like this were included as part of the "well-rounded approach to modern education" offered by the Academy. Swimming, hiking, riding, and golf were all the bait it took to bring Solveig to the surface like a hungry fish after a mosquito, to make her work, early and late, for excellence in every class.

And once I got here, she reflected sourly, the one thing I wanted most was to get a chance—one single solitary chance —to ride Snake Dancer. I didn't want to pitch a no-hitter. I didn't want to play the guitar for the Sing or win the fifty-yard dash. I just wanted to ride Snake Dancer. Was that too much to ask?

She turned to look out the bus window at the one good horse the camp boasted. He stood at the end of the corral— not too tall (he was a quarter horse), powerful, with a deep chest and broad barrel. He was sable-brown, and his coat gleamed in the late-afternoon sun. He had a fine, sensitive head and a spirit not yet ruined by careless handling and incompetent riders. Some of the girls thought he had come from Wyoming, others from Idaho or Arizona.

His name was said to have been given to him because, like all well-trained quarter horses, he could switch directions so suddenly. "Turn on a nickel and give you some change," old

3

Sandoz, the riding master and horse wrangler, called it. Solveig knew he was incredibly fast and agile; no wonder they called him Snake Dancer. He could change directions effortlessly, just like the graceful Indians of the southwest when they performed the Snake Dance. Snake Dancer—free, strong, and brave, as out of place here as a captive Indian war chief.

The horse was new to the camp, having been brought there in the last few weeks by Kramer, who had a contract with the camp to supply them with horses. But Kramer muttered sourly as soon as the girls thronged around Snake Dancer, and Sandoz was equally reluctant to let anyone mount him. It was generally understood that he was "too much horse" for kids, and only one or two of the oldest girls were allowed to ride him, and then just for short canters around the perimeter of the playing fields.

Even the fact that Solveig had a horse of her own, a sleek brown gelding named Jubilee, kept at a boarding farm at home, was not enough to persuade Sandoz to let her ride the big brown horse. Every day Solveig dashed out to the stable, only to be given a fat, dull pony to plod around on, and every day she ate her heart out and resolved to get her hands on Snake Dancer, somehow.

If only I could run over there now and saddle and bridle him. And ride—all my myself—just Snake Dancer and me—

Suddenly there was a sharp cry at the front of the bus. Miss P was struggling and shrieking. Solveig heard screams of "Mouse! Purse!"—and realized someone had succeeded in pulling off that hairy old joke of slipping the carcass of a dead mouse into the headmistress's purse. Everyone jumped up, stretching and craning to see. Laughter, shouts, delighted confusion rocked the bus.

Solveig stood glumly beside the emergency exit. Snake

4

Dancer seemed to be watching her . . . waiting for her to do something. . . .

Almost without her being aware of it, her hand reached out—depressed the lever on the door. It swung open easily, silently. Without a sound she grabbed her duffel bag and slipped through the door. It clicked shut behind her and she was suddenly standing on the tarmac of the loading zone. The October air snapped and the ground felt good under her feet.

Snake Dancer nickered. He was watching her.

They'll see me—Miss P will know I've gotten off the bus, was her first thought.

But she was completely hidden back here. All the cars carrying departing camp personnel were on the opposite side of the bus. And now the shrieking and laughter were subsiding as Miss P evidently regained her composure. In a moment order would be restored, the driver would let in the clutch, and the bus for Coldbrook Academy would roll down the drive.

It's a joke, she heard herself say clearly as she stepped over into the bushes. I'm just playing a joke. Boy, will they be mad when they get a couple of miles down the road and find I'm not on the bus. She could see Miss P's red face getting redder, hear the laughter of the girls when the driver had to halt the bus and turn it around and come back to get her.

I'll think up a story, she snorted, as the bushes by the loading area closed around her. I'll say I was attacked and pulled off the bus my a masked man who held a gun at my head. That'll drive old Miss P right out of her skull—

The bus engine roared, and clouds of blue smoke belched from the exhaust as the bus started to roll. Solveig peered eagerly through the cover of leaves as it began to move slowly, picked up speed, gears shifting. Its square yellow rear end turned the curve onto the dirt road and suddenly winked out, lost among the trees that crowded thickly between the camp and the state highway twenty-five miles away.

And now, she thought in the sudden ecstatic silence left behind the bus—and now for a brisk canter on Snake Dancer before they find out I'm not on the bus and come back to get me—

Chapter 2

SHE LEFT her duffel bag in the bushes. It was a beast to carry because she always kept it half full of horse magazines to read when things got dull. No use to haul it far from the loading zone because there was no doubt in her mind that the bus would be back in a few minutes. Miss P had a passion for roll-calling, which she did in subtle ways: "Jones, have you written your mother this week? Kemper, how is your research paper coming? Longrigg, I dropped my pen—have you seen it?" It was only a matter of time until her restless eye looked for Nilsson and she discovered that Nilsson was not there. Meanwhile—back at the ranch—

Solveig was glad she had decided to wear her jeans and her new pink sweat shirt for the trip home; they would be good to ride in. It was lucky, too, that she had cowboy boots on instead of the tennis shoes she usually wore. It was easier to keep a good seat in the saddle with boots to give you firm footing in the stirrups. So all systems were "go."

The tack room was locked, of course, but Solveig just happened to know about a loose board on the side that overlooked the corral. Solveig just happened to know about quite a number of loose boards, locks that didn't catch, hinges that looked solid but could be pulled out of the rotten wood. Such items of information were common stock around schools, camps, and playgrounds—anyplace where a lot of kids spend a lot of time. The knowledge of one loose board could save you a lot of time in dealing with the adult world.

There was no electricity, of course, since the camp was now closed for the season, but once inside the tack room she could see well enough to find a rope, western saddle, blanket, and bridle. It was hard getting the saddle through the gap behind the loose board, but she managed to work it out sideways. All the time she was listening for the roar of the bus—she had no way to know how soon they would miss her and start back.

There were eleven horses in the corral and her presence seemed to make them nervous. Not that the ten fat ponies did much—just shuffled slowly around, stirring up dust and flies and keeping barely out of her reach. But Snake Dancer snorted and stamped and wheeled briskly and displayed a smart skill in keeping all the other horses between himself and her. Plodding after him with the rope in her hand, she was almost ready to give up the whole crazy idea when a lucky throw (practiced for hours on her horse at home) settled the rope over his neck. The other horses drifted away.

Solveig stood with the end of the rope in her hand, staring up at Snake Dancer. For a moment, in the silence of the deserted camp, she was gripped by a faint uneasiness. Snake Dancer was big and powerful. Every muscle bulged with disciplined strength and it now occurred to her to wonder if he was vicious—if he kicked or bit. She was a good rider (even if they didn't believe her) but she had never been allowed to ride this horse before. *Was* she good enough to handle him?

He could easily trample her underfoot, break every bone she had. Her heart began to beat harder, thudding in her chest. It was one thing to flout Miss P and jump off the bus, to plan a last glorious ride on the camp's prize horse, but now here she stood looking up—*way* up—at him.

"Jeez," she muttered. "What if—what if he throws me?" She could feel a little trickle of sweat creeping down between her shoulder blades. If Snake Dancer threw her she would be alone till the bus came back, with whatever damage the horse could do . . . and some considerable explanations to make to Miss P, although it was a little late to think of that now.

"Well," she pushed all thought of compound fractures out of her mind, "this is what I came back here to do."

She tugged on the rope and Snake Dancer came forward. She tied him up snugly to the corral fence and picked up the saddle blanket. As she stepped up to put it on him, Snake Dancer swiveled around. He thrust his head out and snuffed the blanket suspiciously. His ears twitched. Only after he had examined it carefully was Solveig allowed to put the saddle blanket in place. She picked up the saddle: it was heavy, even though it was a small one, but before she could hoist it up to his back, Snake Dancer had to sniff it all over too.

"What's the matter," Solveig panted, with the saddle raised to shoulder height where the horn could dig into her neck and the stirrup bang her on the knee, "haven't you ever seen a saddle before?"

Snake Dancer snorted. Solveig finally got the saddle up on him, but she was puffing and red in the face by the time she had the cinch fastened. (She had once timed herself saddling and bridling Jubilee at home. Three minutes. Flat.)

That left the bridle. Snake Dancer's head was far out of reach and he now seemed to be stretching his neck up like the boom on a crane so his eyes and ears could take in sights and sounds from the darkening woods beyond the fence. The saddle creaked as he swung his head restlessly back and forth, and he drew in deep breaths of air and snorted them out as if he were seeking for a special scent. Once he narrowly missed stepping on her foot, and she was glad again that she had boots on instead of tennis shoes.

Solveig took the top of the bridle in her right hand and the bit in her left and raised it. Immediately Snake Dancer's head snapped up to a beautiful alert pose, ears forward. After a short struggle she lowered the bridle. Snake Dancer's head drooped. Solveig raised the bridle. Snake Dancer's head jerked up. Down with the bridle, down with the head. Up with the bridle, up with the head.

Solveig started to smolder. They were wasting too much time. "Okay, if you want to play dirty," she muttered, "I'll fix *you*."

She climbed up on the corral fence and wrapped her legs around a tall post, leaned far out, and slipped the bridle on while Snake Dancer was busy watching something on the other side of the corral. As she buckled the cheek strap, Snake Dancer chewed the bit and laid his ears back. Solveig glared. "Listen, crow bait, we're wasting time!"

At last the horse was ready. The sun was nearly down now but there should be time for a quick ride—she still couldn't hear the bus coming back. With a little luck she would be able to have a wonderful gallop—down the road and into the trees, around the lake on the Fire Flower Trail, up the hill north of the dorm and then back to the corral—before Miss P worked her way through the alphabet and back to the letter N again.

The heavy gate swung open and Snake Dancer stepped

through, almost treading on her heels. She pushed the gate shut hurriedly so the other horses wouldn't get out—no sense creating a stampede.

Now. Now it was time to mount Snake Dancer.

She stared up at the horse, and once again felt a little wisp of fear creep over her. He was so big. Powerful. Fast. Locked in that brown satin hide was a being strong enough to kill her if he chose to, and smart enough to figure out how to do it. *Was* she good enough to ride him?

A twig snapped somewhere in the woods and Snake Dancer started. So did Solveig. Time was running out. Bus or no bus, it would soon be too dark to ride. It was now or never.

She threw the reins over his head, holding the loop in her left hand, grabbed the stirrup, and shoved her left toe in it. Bouncing hard on her right foot, she started to spring up— and narrowly missed being trampled as Snake Dancer started to bolt. Panic grabbed her as her hand clenched on the reins.

Trembling, with tears just ready to start, Solveig led the horse to a mounting block and crawled up on it. Snake Dancer snorted and looked back, but he stood still as she threw a leg over and eased into the saddle. She settled her feet into the stirrups and gathered up the reins, screwed her rear end into the saddle for a good, firm seat.

It was just as well.

Snake Dancer ran for miles before she could stop him.

Chapter 3

SHE COULD never remember the horse starting to run. One minute she was sitting there getting firmly anchored, tucking in her elbows and chin, and then Snake Dancer exploded like a bullet shot out of a gun.

For the first few seconds she didn't even think. Hauled back on the reins, ducked her head, grabbed the saddle horn. She screamed, although there was no one to scream *to*. Then, as the horse's hooves hit the ground in a pounding rhythm and the cold air streamed by her face in a gale, one thought gripped her: I can't hang on—I'm going to fall—fall—fall—

She struggled to pull back on the reins, but the effort threw her askew and she nearly lost her grip on the saddle horn. It was like trying to thread a needle while you were crashing around inside the funnel of a tornado. What'll—I *do*—can't stop—him—

Snake Dancer had chosen to bolt down the dirt road leading from the stable into the trees. At the edge of the forest the road forked, one track, called the Fire Flower Trail, going right to circle the lake, and the other south into the hills and ending—where, she had no idea. As the horse's wild rush ate

13

up the road, she forced her eyes open. Hoping to turn him, she hauled sharply on the right rein.

But the fork in the road disappeared behind them and Snake Dancer plunged on down the track into the deep forest. His ears were up, his head stretched out, tail flying. Once or twice he broke stride and kicked up his heels. He ran as if he were having the most enormous kind of fun, as if he could run like this forever—

Solveig started to cry. Oh, Lord—what am I going to do? Can't stop him. If I fall off I'll kill myself—

All she could do was hang on. Sooner or later he had to stop. Even a cannonball like Snake Dancer couldn't run forever.

The road turned into a trail where trees grew so close their branches met across it. It twisted and turned in every direction, swung over hills and into gullys, up again over low ridges. Twigs slashed her face and stung her arms and the light was so dim she prayed the horse wouldn't fall. If he fell—

She had no idea how long or how far he ran. They were out of the gentle open valley where the camp was located, well into the forested hills to the south, before she could feel him begin to slow down. But before she had a chance to swing her legs forward and shift her weight back in the saddle, Snake Dancer simply put on the brakes and slammed to a halt. Solveig folded down over the saddle horn and all the air rushed out of her lungs as her rib cage hit the pommel. Her nose and chin crashed into the horse's arched neck and she saw dancing colored stars all over the dark forest. *Glugg* . . . she wobbled up, spitting horse hair and dirt. Oh, wow. Oh, my Lord. Got to watch that. I've got to remember that's why they call him Snake Dancer—because he can stop so fast—

14

For several trembling seconds Solveig sat absolutely still in the saddle. Her left hand was still clenched on the reins, her right on the saddle horn. Her fingers were raw and burning. She felt as if someone had systematically pounded her all over with a baseball bat, bruising her from head to foot.

Snake Dancer stood still, panting so hard that Solveig felt as if she were astride a bellows. The horse's head swung from side to side and his ears flicked forward and back as he examined the dark forest crowding close on each side of them. Then he drew in a deep breath and sneezed it out through loose lips, stretched his neck, and shook his head till the bridle chains rattled. As he shifted his weight from foot to foot, relaxing, Solveig too took a deep, shaky breath.

"Jeez. I'm lost. Miles from camp. In the dark. Don't know where I am. Nobody *else* knows where I am. Miss P gets hold of me, I'll be in solitary for centuries. Mom and Dad—oh, boy—wait'll *they* get to me. But—" she straightened up in the saddle and felt the bruises like red-hot brands "—*I rode him. I rode Snake Dancer on the wildest run he could ever make, and I didn't fall. Maybe now they'll believe me: I'm not stupid, and I'm not lost in the middle of the alphabet. My name is Xenia Y. Zilch, and I can ride Snake Dancer.*

"And it was worth every bit of what it's going to cost me."

By this time she was certain the bus would have returned and Miss P and the driver, possibly assisted by some of the older girls, would be making a search of the dorm, the outbuildings, the lake shore, and playgrounds. They would probably stumble over her duffel bag in the bushes by the loading zone. Her skin crawled when she thought of Miss P grabbing it up in her skinny hands, possibly opening it for a search. Not that there was anything in it that shouldn't have been there—just some rumpled pajamas with two buttons missing, a few old magazines, and her toothpaste wrapped in a plastic bag because she always lost the cap. About the worst thing that could happen would be that Miss P might spot her bottle of anti-fingernail-biting medicine.

Solveig kept it to use when the urge to gnaw her nails down to stubs overcame her. The medicine was about half gone, but, unfortunately, so were her nails. Her fingers were blunt-ended and harassed-looking, and Solveig wondered in despair why she—who had no problems—was a nail biter when people like Jeanne Thompson (alcoholic mother) and Debbie Meyers (two complete sets of parents, plain and step) had hands like Revlon advertisements. In any case, Solveig carried the bottle in dumb hope and from time to time dabbed the vile-tasting stuff on her fingernails, usually just after she had chewed them all down again.

There was a crisp rattling sound off to the left in the dark forest, probably just a pine cone falling through the branches below it. Snake Dancer's head swung toward the sound and then he slowly shifted to face it. Solveig strained her eyes and ears, but the darkness was so thick she might have had a bucket turned down over her head. She had no doubt that Snake Dancer could see quite well, but she certainly could not. The sound was not repeated and both horse and rider relaxed a little.

Now that her head wasn't swinging up and down like a yo-yo and the horse's flanks no longer pumped so hard, Solveig put herself to thinking about how to get back to camp. She had no idea at all where she was, but buried at the back of her mind was the germ of a million-dollar idea. One of the few things she remembered from the instructions given them by camp personnel was a pithy bit of advice from old Sandoz.

16

She had not understood it at all when she heard it, but in the last sixty seconds it had become completely clear: "When you're lost, give the horse his head and he'll always take you home." Nobody, least of all Solveig, had expected one of the well-disciplined Coldbrook girls to take off on a wild ride at night on a runaway horse, but just the same it was a God's mercy that old Sandoz had thrown them that little gem of information.

Now—how to do it? She leaned forward very carefully and slid her hand down the left side of the saddle under the stirrup leathers to the heavy ring where the cinch was fastened. Slipping her fingers under the ring, she pried at it, trying to see if the cinch was still tight enough to hold the saddle for the ride back. Because there was absolutely no hope that she could get off and tighten it here. Snake Dancer would take off like a rocket, or at least not let her mount again, and if that happened she would not only be lost, but afoot, miles from camp. And even with the road to follow, it would be almost impossible to walk back to camp in the dark.

The cinch had loosened somewhat, but she thought it would hold if she could keep Snake Dancer to a walk. Solveig straightened up and got a good grip on the reins, but left them loose enough so the horse was free to choose his own direction. She pressed her heels very lightly into his sides, and gripped the saddle horn.

Snake Dancer swung around, snorted two or three times, and kicked once. Her heart lurched. Then he stretched his head out down what she hoped would be the trail back to camp and took a few tentative steps. Behind them another rattle broke the stillness. Solveig shivered. Snake Dancer shivered. And then Snake Dancer started walking, an easy, comfortable, swinging walk. All she had to do now was hang on.

The trip back to camp naturally took much longer than the headlong stampede coming out. Solveig tried to figure out what time it might be now, since it was too dark to see her watch. It had been about five-thirty when the bus was loading for the trip back to the Academy. Allowing for maybe thirty minutes to catch and saddle Snake Dancer, then fifteen or twenty minutes—half an hour?—when he bolted with her, and an hour or more to get back to camp at his now deliberate pace, it would be something like seven-thirty before she could get there. The only good thing she could think of was that, after so long a time, she was certain the bus and Miss P would be there to meet her. Alone now in the dark forest, she suddenly began to find this prospect appealing.

Although she couldn't see the trail, the forest, or the hills around her, Solveig could look straight up and see stars, and by watching them could tell that the trail wound back and forth as it dropped into the valley. The constellations of Pegasus, Pisces, and Aries were first ahead, then off to her right, then behind her shoulder. Watching the stars wheeling around overhead made her dizzy. Best to hang on, close her eyes, and try to think of something to say to Miss P.

It was a real challenge. She could be mysterious: "It was—something I *had* to do." Breezy? "Miss P, I presume?" Contrite: "Oh, I'm *so* sorry to have upset you, Miss P." Honest: "You wouldn't believe me when I said I could ride Snake Dancer, so I just had to show you I could do it!" There was no question in her mind but that honesty was the best policy, but there *was* a question as to whether or not she was strong enough to adopt that policy. Miss P had a way of making you wish you were either totally truthful or a highly skilled liar.

With the problem of her explanation still unresolved, she began to be aware that the trail was coming to an end. The

18

ground no longer sloped downward; Snake Dancer's body under her was level, not pitching forward at the withers, and she sensed that the trees were thinning. Any minute now she would begin to catch a glimpse of lights at the camp and hear voices calling her name. Wearily she acknowledged that both would be welcome, even the sight of Miss P and her red neck and white collar. Anything would be better than these black woods, and the soft, stealthy sounds. . . .

As she rounded the last bend and the trees between her and the camp thinned, she saw a flash of light. Closer than I thought, she murmured, and involuntarily pulled Snake Dancer to a halt. Might as well enjoy the full drama of the moment—it would be quite a while before she would be seeing any excitement after this episode.

But there was something wrong.

It was a truck backed up beside the dorm—not a bus. And those figures running around in the harsh glare of its head-lights—they weren't Miss P, the bus driver, the girls. They were men—four of them. And they were fighting. She could hear a ragged shout: "You lost him, you fool! You *lost* him— I'll get you for this!"

As Solveig watched, transfixed, one of the men raised his fist and smashed it into another man's face. The second figure dropped to the ground. A third turned and started to run. Instantly the first man raised a black stick to his shoulder and a sound like a shot rang out. A *black stick*?

Oh, jeez.

It's not a stick.

It's a gun.

Chapter 4

SOLVEIG had no idea of how long she sat there, glued to Snake Dancer's back like a forgotten Band-Aid. She heard the rifle go off—they must have heard that sound clear to Africa—and watched, frozen, as the man dropped. But after a few seconds he sat up, then crawled slowly to his feet. The man with the gun now held it ready, but pointing downward a little, and the other three people milled around in front of him. At this distance Solveig could hear only scattered sounds, since they were no longer shouting, but couldn't make any sense out of them. Dust kicked up by their boots drifted in low white clouds across the beams of the truck headlights, further obscuring the scene.

One thing was clear: whatever was going on at the camp, it was nothing Solveig wanted to get mixed up in. I'm in enough trouble already, she thought, in a brief moment of frenzy as she stared at the bizarre scene framed between the crescent-shaped curves of Snake Dancer's ears. I sure don't need any more.

She turned and searched the darkness that concealed the stretch of road down which the bus had disappeared several

hours ago. Surely its headlights would appear there any second. But the road, a crooked slash through the pine forest, was empty and dark. She listened for the telltale rattle of bus wheels crossing the bridge. The shallow Cottonwood River was no more than half a mile east of the camp and, when it was quiet, you could always hear any vehicle cross the wooden bridge long before you could see it. "I'd give anything to see that rotten old bus show up right now," she groaned. "I'd even be glad to see Miss P."

But all that had come to the camp at this late hour was a truck. And four men. And a gun.

Snake Dancer snorted and stamped, and suddenly Solveig remembered something. Horses liked to call to each other. She was sure that wasn't the right way to say it, but she had always observed that when a horse approached camp and saw the other horses in the corral, he would set up a friendly nickering, and those in the corral would answer back. Any minute now one of the horses in the corral—or Snake Dancer—was going to sound off. Snake Dancer's head was up with his ears flicking forward; he could easily see the other horses milling around in the corral—the truck was parked so its lights shone directly on them. If he let out a whinny, the strangers at the camp would know another horse—possibly with a rider—was out there, and they just might decide to investigate.

The first thing to do was retreat—get back far enough so that Snake Dancer couldn't give their presence away. Solveig had no idea what she was going to do, but she was clear on one thing: she intended to stay as far as possible from four men who shouted, cursed, fought, and shot at each other.

She lifted Snake Dancer's reins and started to turn him back onto the trail over which he had just come. But Snake Dancer balked, swung his head back toward the camp, and yanked stubbornly against the bit. He was plainly set on going back to the stable where he knew there would be hay, water, and the company of other horses. He lurched and kicked, and Solveig lurched too, knowing he could easily pitch her off into the weeds. And if he did that, he would immediately take off again and she would be completely alone and helpless there in the dark.

"Ho, boy, ho—" She patted his shoulder as the horse began to curvet. "*I'm* in charge here," she lied, "and we're going back into the trees."

Snake Dancer turned, stopped, looked back at the camp. Solveig decided on desperate measures—she slapped him lightly with the ends of the reins. He snorted and stamped and broke into an electric tap dance, swinging head and tail back and forth. Solveig gripped the saddle horn, scrunched up her face, and clapped her heels into his ribs. Snake Dancer snorted again, cranked his head back to stare longingly over his shoulder, and then, dragging one foot after the other, began to slowly shuffle back toward the woods. His gait was halting; he limped.

"Put-on!" muttered Solveig furiously. "You big *put-on*! You can run forty miles when *you* want to go, but when *I* want you to go, all at once you've gone lame!"

Losing her temper, she slapped him smartly with the reins. Startled, Snake Dancer sprang forward and for one horrible moment she wondered if she had touched off another runaway. But after two or three strides, Snake Dancer slowed to a jolting trot, although he still swung his head to stare regretfully back at the camp.

After urging the horse back up the trail and into the trees where he could no longer see the stable (and it was absolutely and terrifyingly dark), Solveig stopped him and sat there for a moment, trying to think. The one thing she didn't want to do was lose the horse. As long as she had him, she felt that she was reasonably safe. On foot she would fall, get lost, certainly could not run away in case the man with the gun happened to decide to shoot *her.*

Solveig's head ached with such crazy thoughts. Nothing in her life had prepared her to consider what to do in case someone started shooting at her. She was enormously tempted to ignore the evidence before her eyes and pretend that what she had just seen had not really happened: things like this *didn't* happen—did they? At least not to people like her.

I'm just plain old Solveig Nilsson. I live at 1481 Columbus Drive and I have nice parents who love me—so far. I have good manners and solid religious training; I get A's in history and I can make square corners on my bed and my puppet show of *Where the Wild Things Are* won a prize last year. But in a fit of temporary insanity, I sneaked off a bus to go for a ride on a horse and now I'm afraid a man with a gun may kill me. How did all this happen? That's the real "Celebrity Sweepstakes" question—how did I get into this? By wanting to be Xenia Y. Zilch and ride Snake Dancer. I was trying to find out if I'm somebody special. I can't blame anybody else for the mess I'm in. I did this all by myself.

And all my myself I've got to figure out how to get out of it.

One thing was clear. She couldn't stay where she was. Her brains thumped and clacked as she rattled around inside her head like somebody searching a storeroom for something valuable they'd misplaced. Had to be something, somewhere—

Yes. The shelter.

On a steep ridge overlooking the camp was a place called the shelter. There was a small clearing in the forest with a fire pit, hitching rails, and a lóg structure open on three sides

24

where bales of hay and extra horse tack were kept. A clear, sweet spring trickled out from under a rock so there was plenty of water nearby. But to reach the shelter, she would have to ride up the Fire Flower Trail. It had been given its name because it led to the shelter, where the camp held cookouts, sings, and nature-study programs, and it looped around the lake, up into the hills, and finally onto the steep ridge overlooking the camp. Although it ended at a point actually quite near the camp, it made a wide horseshoe bend of at least five miles.

Solveig swallowed. Another five miles? In the dark? But it was all she could think of. And from the shelter she could easily see the camp below. She loathed the thought of another long trek, through the silent—or not so silent—forest, but it beat sitting here on the back of a horse who might decide to dump her at any time. At the end of the Fire Flower Trail would be water, hay for Snake Dancer, safety for both of them.

And from the shelter, she could watch the camp, the men, and the truck. When they left, she would ride back down and be there when the bus came back.

And the bus *would* come back.

She was sure of that.

Chapter 5

SNAKE DANCER had run off some of his pent-up energy and now went forward at a more reasonable pace. He had a good gait—a long, fast, swinging walk that ate up the miles, and he seemed to be able to see in the dark, although he shied now and then as the wind rattled a clump of brush or a stone rolled under his hoof. He had never been over the Fire Flower Trail as far as she knew, but Solveig could feel him instinctively selecting the smoothest ground, swinging wide around boulders and trees along the edge. She had been in the dark for so long that she had begun to see a little, although the light from the stars was as faint as silver powder dusted over the earth. But no matter how she watched and listened, it was clear that the horse's senses were much sharper than hers; he could see, smell, hear things that were totally lost to her. All the more reason to make sure that nothing separated her from the horse.

As the road started to turn north, she could look back and catch glimpses through the trees of the area illuminated by the truck's headlights. The fight seemed to have ended. All four men now stood in the light and there were no more gun shots. It seemed that whatever had caused the disturbance was over and they were only talking. Now the trail led through a grove of pine trees and the camp was out of sight for a few minutes. Then, from higher ground, she saw it again. This would be the last time she could see the camp clearly until she reached the shelter on the ridge. She pulled Snake Dancer up and sat for a moment, chilled and bone-weary, staring down.

Suddenly the truck lights went out.

Baffled, Solveig blinked. The truck should have been driven away if the invaders had decided to leave. If so, the lights would have changed position, probably backed up as the truck was headed around and into the road, and then she would have seen the tail lights go down the road, through the forest, over the bridge, and disappear, the way the bus had.

But that had not happened. The lights had just gone out.

That meant the truck was still there. And that the men had decided to stay.

Solveig groaned. She had been counting on being able to wait it out—stay hidden in the forest until whatever was happening at the camp was concluded and she could safely return. Although she expected the bus to reappear at any moment, until it did she was convinced that the men represented a clear danger that she would have to avoid. Having them at the camp would make it a little harder to reach the bus when it came back, although not impossible. Thinking it all over, she felt she ought to be able to come down from the high ridge where the shelter was located to the camp by a more direct route, rather than having to ride all the way back around the Fire Flower Trail. There had been talk of another trail, steep, rocky, dangerous, down from the ridge, although she had never seen it. Certainly she could not locate the trail—if it existed—in the dark, or ride down it if she did. That would have to wait for morning.

Well, in any case, all thought of return to camp tonight was what Miss P called an *academic question*. That meant it didn't do you any good to worry about something because you couldn't do it any how. Nothing to do now but push on to the shelter and make the best of it.

It must have taken an hour or more to reach the ridge. Solveig was so tired and cold that her feet and legs were numb, her fingers frozen around the reins when the trees suddenly opened up at the top of the last steep pitch and Snake Dancer's hooves struck the hard-packed earth of the clearing.

I've got to get off, she thought dizzily. I don't care if he does run away. I've got to get off.

Solveig leaned forward, swung her right leg back over the saddle, and as her weight shifted there was a sliding rush and the saddle rolled sideways under her.

She hit the ground like a ripe pumpkin with the saddle on top of her.

Oh, jeez. If Sandoz could see me now.

Half-stunned, she lay there looking up at the dark blotch that was Snake Dancer's belly. Praying that he wouldn't pick up a foot and lay it down on her face, she rolled carefully over and inched backward. Her left foot was clear through the stirrup and the saddle horn dug into her stomach. There was no way to get clear of the thing; she could only drag it with her. At last she was out from under the horse and able to work her foot and leg out through the stirrup. As she wobbled slowly to her feet, Snake Dancer turned his head and put out his muzzle. He sniffed her deliberately from head to

foot and let out a long, rattling snort of what sounded like bottomless contempt.

Yeah. Me, too, thought Solveig drearily. Only good thing about it is that nobody saw me when it happened. Last girl who let a saddle turn on her at Camp Ahwanee was grounded for a whole day and had to shovel three wheelbarrow-loads of dung onto the camp's manure pile.

She picked up the saddle and clutching the reins (which she had somehow held onto all this time), she stumbled toward the shelter. Dark, cold, open on one side, empty (she already knew, having been there earlier on a field trip), except for some bales of hay and a few odd pieces of rope, an old bucket, some bits of wood and camp gear—still, the shelter would be like heaven after the long dark ride.

I need some rest, she thought as she tied Snake Dancer to one of the hitching posts by the bridle reins. In the morning I'll figure out what to do.

Chapter 6

SOLVEIG pulled a block of hay off the open end of a bale and put it on the ground by Snake Dancer so he could feed. She knew he wouldn't like eating with the bridle on, but in the dark she couldn't locate a halter or a rope, although she was sure she had seen both the other day, hanging on the walls of the shelter. Snake Dancer snorted a few times, thrashed the hay around, and then settled to a steady, comfortable munching.

She hoped he didn't need water too badly. There was a spring nearby, but in the darkness she felt she would not be able to find it without falling in. She checked the knot in Snake Dancer's reins one more time and then crept back into the shelter. There was a spot where several bales of hay were piled with a space between them; if she crawled in there and pulled some loose hay over her like a blanket, maybe she could keep warm enough to sleep.

With the hay rustling like a feathery comforter over her, Solveig lay looking up at the darkness of the shelter roof. She could see only a tiny patch of sky now, and the stars looked icy, like the first points of frost on a winter's night. For a while she tried to think, calmly and reasonably. About Miss P and the bus: something astonishing and unforeseeable had prevented Miss P from becoming aware of her absence by now.

Only an emergency of the first magnitude would cause Miss P's radar to be turned off, and now there was no telling when it would be turned on again. Miss P was the prime mover who kept the school functioning, the kingpin, the energizer. Without her to goad them, the others—especially the girls—would lie down right next to an erupting volcano and go to sleep. So, instead of expecting the bus back within minutes or at the most an hour or two, as she originally had, Solveig now realized that she ought to face the fact that it could be—hours? *Days?*

So all right. Think about the situation at the camp: for some reason unknown to her, four men (and a gun) had come to the camp and were fighting violently among themselves. As far as she knew, the only person who should be coming to the camp—probably tomorrow morning—was Kramer. He should be picking up his horses tomorrow sometime. But Kramer wouldn't spend money to hire a van just to move eleven horses a distance of twenty-five miles: he would probably have some of his hired hands ride and drive them. So the men at the camp weren't Kramer and his men. And if they weren't Kramer's men, who were they? And why did one of them try to shoot another?

All she could do, finally, was promise herself that she would try to find out tomorrow—when it was daylight—what was going on.

And at last she slept.

Once during the night something rustled in the forest at the edge of the clearing, and she woke up, heart pounding. Her eyes strained to see in the darkness as great waves of fear slid over her like a tide coming in. She lay listening for several minutes but there was no further sound, and Snake Dancer did not appear to be alarmed. He stood, head down, his left hind leg kinked and resting on the rim of the hoof; he was sleeping, mostly on his feet, as all horses do.

The moon had risen very late in the night but the light slanting into the clearing seemed only to make the forest darker than before. The shadows were so densely black in contrast to the silvery light from the moon, that now she could not see anything at all. She turned over very quietly so she could face outward and watch the clearing. If anything approached, she would be ready.

Ready for *what*? I couldn't fight off a chipmunk or a wood-pecker. What'll I do if a bear walks out of those woods, or a cougar? She knew quite well (in the top half of her head, where her algebra, geography, TV schedules, and common sense were stored), that neither a bear nor a cougar was going to slink across that stretch of bare ground. But (in the bottom half of her head, where she kept old nightmares, suspicions, half-truths, and myths), she also knew that *anything* could materialize out of that primeval darkness. Fear, if nothing else, would make it so.

That's why, she thought bleakly, people like me are told to avoid strangers, get home before dark, and are sent to camp in the care of responsible people like Miss P.

Where did I go wrong?

Only this afternoon I was a nice quiet girl in a safe place—smack in the middle of the alphabet—and now here I am all alone on a mountain in the dark, and the nearest neighbors are outlaws. Worst of all—I didn't *fall* into trouble. I jumped. Nobody to blame but S. Nilsson. Just because I wanted to ride

Snake Dancer, I climbed off the bus into an awful lot of trouble. Kind of thing you see in an adventure movie on TV where some ten-year-old kid with buck teeth solves the murder or rescues a whole town from fire and flood. Brave, clear-eyed, impulsive—

I think I've been oversold on impulsiveness.

Chapter 7

WHEN SHE AWOKE it was not yet fully daylight. Inside the shelter it was still shadowy and half dark, and for a moment Solveig lay still and stared about her, puzzled. Then she tried to roll over, and the hay rustled. Her stiff joints screamed, and she remembered where she was.

Her first clear thought was for Snake Dancer. She scrambled up and staggered out of the shelter. Yes, there he was. He was snorting and stamping and his restless hooves had cut the dry, hard ground up as if it had been plowed, but he was there.

For a moment she stared at him as he stood there with his fine head up, his powerful neck arched above his deep chest. Short-coupled and strong, muscular without being gross, Snake Dancer showed generations of careful breeding. He was a fine horse. No, he was more than that. Snake Dancer was the kind of horse you saw in pictures, in competitions, at horse shows. From years of earnest study, Solveig knew enough about horses to realize that Snake Dancer was one of the finest quarter horses anyone had ever seen, and from personal, bruising experience that he was probably one of the fastest.

The only odd thing about him was his color. In a world full of bay, black, sorrel, and white horses, Snake Dancer was a clear, deep, sable brown with a faint dapple pattern on his flanks that reminded Solveig of transparent bubbles floating on dark water. A narrow, crooked white blaze streaked down his face and his left fore leg was splashed with white as if he had accidentally set his foot down in a bucket of paint, but every other hair on his polished hide was of a uniformly mahogany brown color. Even his mane and tail, usually black on a horse of his color, were sable brown. Solveig could not remember ever having seen a horse with Snake Dancer's markings and color.

Snake Dancer put his head down and snorted, blowing up a cloud of dust from the ground. Solveig knew he must be thirsty and terribly restless from having the bridle on and being tied up all night. Shivering in the chill morning air, she untied the reins and led him around the shelter into the edge of the trees to the spring. But when he stood by the clear little pool, instead of taking a dainty drink, Snake Dancer dipped his muzzle into the water and then wagged his head violently forward and back, like a paddle being stroked furiously, splashing water in all directions. Solveig cringed as the icy water spattered over her legs and feet.

"Cripes!" she shrieked. "What are you doing?"

But having thoroughly soaked her boots and jeans, Snake Dancer now stood still and drank tranquilly, sipping clear water through his soft gray lips. Two or three times he raised his head, chewing and flapping and streaming gouts of water down into the pool and over her feet, when he turned to rub his head against her shoulder. Reeling on the edge of the

pool, Solveig clutched the bridle and tried to fight off his rubbing and slobbering.

"Holy torpedo juice," she moaned. "Why can't you just drink the water? How come you've got to spray it all over me *too*?"

A blue jay flashed through the trees, calling shrilly, and instantly Snake Dancer's head snapped up, nearly pulling her arm out of its socket. He followed the flight of the bird with great interest, his neck weaving effortlessly from side to side, while Solveig, still holding the bridle reins, dangled like a yo-yo. Snake Dancer looked carefully over each shoulder, ears wigwagging, kicked two or three times, and finally shook himself all over.

Another drink. More splashing, more slobbering. Finally, finished with the water, he backed away. Solveig led him back to the hitching rail. She was wet to the knees and had two new bruises where his head had struck her shoulder. Coming to Camp Ahwanee, she mused, was to have been a learning experience, according to Miss P. And, *boy,* has it ever been. Taking this horse to water is a real experience, and I learned a lot from it. Next time I'll wear gum boots, carry an umbrella and a sponge, and use a forty-foot rope so I can stand clear of him.

Back at the shelter she located a halter that would fit Snake Dancer and a long rope to tie him up with. There was a small patch of fresh grass just into the trees, and she tied him there, with careful attention to the knots. She threw down a little more hay to keep him fully occupied in case the grass gave out. Listening to him eat, she realized that her own stomach was empty and growling. Oh, for a stack of hot cakes, a glass of milk, even a bowl of cold cereal. She wondered drearily how long it took a person to starve to death. There would be an inquest, of course, when her emaciated body was finally found, and she hoped Miss P would spend eternity in jail regretting her failure to check out the absence of one Solveig Nilsson from her rotten old bus.

Solveig's stomach rumbled again. What would Xenia Y. Zilch do in a case like this?

Chapter 8

THE CAMP—and food, food, food—was not really very far away, a fact she had known when she set out for the shelter last night. After making sure again that Snake Dancer was safely tethered, Solveig made her way through the trees to a lookout point a few yards below the shelter. Time to be thinking about the next move.

The view from the lookout point was fantastic. On all sides, jagged ranges of mountains stretched as far as she could see, with forested ridges and bald rocky domes rippling like a great, frozen, green sea. Directly below her was the shallow valley at the west end of which the camp was located. Eastward the river meandered along in a series of loops to the point where it escaped the valley by means of a rocky canyon. The river's course was marked by flashes of yellow where willow and cottonwood trees were turning autumn colors. She could even see the old wooden bridge and the sparkle of the water tumbling over the stony bed beneath it.

The camp itself seemed quiet and peaceful as the rising sun's rays slanted across the baseball field, the corral, and the lawns. The main dormitory appeared from here to be locked and shuttered, but Solveig knew there was a window on the second floor over the veranda that could be opened easily. It was a well-kept secret, passed down from one group of campers to the next by way of slips of paper left in discrete places, and the window, which had been broken probably for years, had continued to be a safety valve for girls who wanted to slip out for one more moonlit walk after curfew, or a sandwich from the cookhouse pantry after a meal of corned beef and cabbage.

The cookhouse was not as secure as it looked, either, although much harder to break into because of its exposed location. However, there was a loose board at the back where a woodshed sheltered the supply of fireplace wood, and once you were in the woodshed, it was a simple matter to pick the lock of the back door and slip into the main camp kitchen. Solveig knew there should be a good supply of canned goods on the shelves there. The camp was usually opened again during the winter for a short season of snow sports, and some basic supplies were always kept there.

If she could just slip in and out of the camp, unseen by the strangers, Solveig felt she could probably handle the food problem, and also gather up some matches for a fire, and maybe an extra coat or even a blanket in case she had to sleep out another night. She would have to go back to the camp on foot, though. On foot she could slip through the trees, from bush to bush, hiding quickly if necessary. Taking Snake Dancer would be like charging into the camp on a fire engine with bells clanging and siren howling. No, this was a job for feet and legs. Lucky mine are strong, she thought. Strong back, weak mind—

The van was nowhere in sight and it must have been driven away during the night, because there was no building at the camp large enough to hide it in. Solveig, peering through the fringe of bushes at the lookout point, could not see any of the men, and there was no smoke spiraling up from any of the chimneys. But there were a number of things that indicated the men were still somewhere about: a half-open gate that had been closed last night, two or three piles of gear left lying near the corral fence, a red coat hanging on a fencepost. She would like to persuade herself that they were gone, and would also have liked to think that even if they were here, they would be no threat to her. But there was the gun—

I'd be stupid to just go charging down there after what happened last night without trying to find out what's going on first. People who do things like that end up on slabs in the mortuary. So it looks like a job for Xenia Y. Zilch, girl hero.

Solveig hurried back to check Snake Dancer and made sure his rope was firmly tied. Snake Dancer snorted and kicked. He was restless at having to be confined, and Solveig gave him some more hay. Fortunately, this seemed to distract him from mischief. Then she got a drink at the spring, checked the clearing and the shelter to make sure there was nothing amiss there, and went back down to the lookout point. She had already discovered that the shorter trail back to the camp led down from the point, that it was steep and rocky, and that she would probably fall most of the way down.

But as hard as it was getting to the bottom of the trail, she wondered, when she got there, how she would ever get back up to the shelter. She guessed it must have taken close to an hour to slide, bump, stumble, and fall down the steep path, with its dozens of switchbacks and steps cut out of solid rock, to where it ended in a patch of dense woods north of the dorm. But returning to the shelter, where Snake Dancer was tethered, would take at least twice as long.

Searching once more for the bus—which was nowhere in sight—she moved cautiously forward. She had decided to stay out of sight until she was sure all the men had gone away. If it made her feel silly, skulking along through the woods, she preferred to feel silly rather than find herself staring into the end of a gun barrel. And all *this,* she muttered grimly, just because I *had* to ride one special horse.

From the foot of the ridge she could move forward through a strip of forest that bordered the baseball field and the tennis courts and track. From the edge of the trees it was easy to dodge from bush to bush, shinny up the wall next to the front veranda where there were trellises for climbing roses, and tiptoe across the roof. Prying open the defective window took only a second; in a moment she dropped quietly into the northeast dorm on the second floor.

The first thing to do was take off her boots. Just in case one of the men might be somewhere in the building, she would have to be very quiet. Then, with the boots under her arm, slowly and carefully she began a tour of the main building.

When she reached the ground floor and the big common room with its scattered couches and chairs and the stone fireplace six kids could stand up in, the first thing that hit her eye was—of course—the telephone. It was an old-fashioned wall phone hung in an alcove with a pile of tattered phone books under it. It was a pay phone provided for guests who were either homesick or financially embarrassed, and needed to call home.

Seeing the phone, Solveig let out a sigh like a gust of wind. Phone! Of course. I'll call Mom and Dad. They'll know what happened by now—probably they're already on the way here to get me. But if they are, they will have left Aunt Jessie at home to answer the phone. Boy, am I glad I've got a dime—

She fished the only coin she had out of her pocket and sprinted across the room. One more minute and she would hear Aunt Jessie's scratchy old voice asking why for mercy sake was she still at the camp when all the other girls were safely back at Coldbrook? One more minute and the whole crazy adventure would be coming to a close.

Solveig lifted the phone off the hook, dropped in her dime, and dialed 0 for Operator.

But instead of the clean, metallic hum of live wires and the brisk voice of the operator, there was a dead, woolly silence. She jiggled the hook. Her dime did not come back.

The phone was dead.

Slowly, her mouth twitching, Solveig hung up the phone. Suddenly she remembered that there was another phone in the director's office that opened onto the front hall. She ran to the office, skidded across the bare floor, and grabbed up the other phone. Dead.

So that was that. The end of the big plan. No phone, no rescue.

Solveig tried hard to put the phones out of her mind. She vowed not to let herself be distracted by the disappointment, and went on with her search as if—almost as if—nothing had happened.

Back upstairs in the dorm, Solveig sat down for a moment to think while she pulled her boots back on. If worst came to worst she might have to camp out again tonight, and if that happened, she wanted to be more comfortable. She tiptoed to a closet (even though she knew this building, at least, was empty except for herself), and lifted out two heavy wool blankets and carried them to the window. It was a little harder getting out and down to the ground with the blankets, but in a few minutes she had them safely stashed in a hidden spot among the pines.

Next stop, the cookhouse. Keeping to the fringe of the trees, she moved around to the back where the woodshed was located. The loose board swung easily and in a couple of seconds she was gently turning the tumblers in the lock with a bent paper clip which was kept (by the girls) in a handy, hidden spot nearby.

But once inside the kitchen hunger overcame her caution. She abandoned further searching until she could find a box of cereal, open a can of milk, and wolf down two bowls of Corn Flakes in quick succession. There was a lot of food here—canned fruit, milk, soup, meat, vegetables—and there would be no problem getting enough to eat, although it wasn't going to be easy to carry. She settled on cereal, canned milk, small cans of peaches, and some square cans of luncheon meat. Adding a can opener, tin bowl and spoon, a box of matches, and a couple of sheets of plastic that looked handy, she loaded it all into an empty knapsack she found in the lean-to. Leaving the cookhouse, she carried the pack back to where she had hidden the blankets.

She decided to finish searching the outbuildings before going back up the trail to the shelter. She had already settled in her mind that she would simply hide out there, and when the bus came back or a familiar search party arrived (Miss P? Her parents?), she would hustle down to meet them.

Oddly, she found that the stable was not only unlocked, but the door was wide open. She slipped in and looked around. It seemed empty, but the horses in the corral were restless and snorty, as if there was someone nearby. Solveig stepped back into the heavy shadows behind a pile of baled hay to look at the bridles hanging there, and suddenly froze.

She could hear voices. Two men were standing just outside the corral fence looking at the horses.

Biting her lip, Solveig sank quietly down behind the hay bales and listened, barely breathing, struggling to make out the words.

"—going to raise cain if we don't find him!"

"How'd *I* know the lousy horse wouldn't be here?" That voice—it sounded familiar!

"You were supposed to *watch* Snake Dancer! That's what the boss paid you for—to watch him. Be sure he was here when we come to get him!"

"But—I—"

"Look here—" there was a choked scuffle and the sound of boots scraping the ground "—you didn't sell him off to somebody else, did you?"

"No! No! Why'd I do—a thing—like *that*?"

"Because Snake Dancer's worth a bundle of money, that's why! Any horse that can win the race at Ruidoso without a sweat is worth a pile—and if you—"

"Wait—Kramer—*I* know what Snake Dancer's worth! It was *my* idea to hide him out here after you guys stole him. Why'd I want to sell him out from under you? Why'd I try a thing like that?"

"I don't know. But if you didn't sell him—then where *is* he?"

"I—don't—know."

I do. Solveig shifted carefully, so as to be ready to streak out the back door of the stable the minute they were out of sight. *I* know where he is. Oh, boy, I know a *lot* of things—now—

46

Chapter 9

—EXCEPT what's a Ruidoso?

After the two men (one of whom she had realized with a hot shock was Sandoz, the riding master) had left the corral, still quarreling, Solveig slid out silent as a shadow and vanished by way of the bushes and clumps of ornamental trees.

When she got back to the spot where the blankets and canned goods were cached, she crouched down to catch her breath. Securely hidden in a thicket, Solveig felt safe for the moment. She was reasonably sure that there were only two men in the camp at the moment, and she had watched them start walking down the road that led to the highway. They were looking for Snake Dancer, and she was momentarily relieved that they were headed in exactly the wrong direction. Watching them go, her eyes fell on the bus loading area and suddenly she remembered that she had hidden her duffel in the bushes there when she had slipped off the bus. What if they found it? Oh, wow—

She knew she didn't have much time. Sliding through the trees, she paused at the edge of the driveway, took a deep breath, streaked down to the loading zone, plowed into the bushes, found the duffel, and raced back to her supply dump in what must have been record speed.

She had to sit for several moments to catch her breath, and while she sat there, she thought about the things she had learned from Sandoz and the man called Kramer.

One thing was absolutely clear. If the invaders were there to steal Snake Dancer, she was going to see to it that they didn't find him. Sooner or later, help would arrive, and when it did she wanted to be able to hand Snake Dancer over to his real owners—whoever they might be. Keeping the horse safe would make up a lot for the foolishness and misery of this silly escapade. No crew of bandits was going to load a treasure like Snake Dancer in a van and disappear with him if she could help it.

If *she* could help it?

Jeez. I'm not Xenia Y. Zilch. I'm a plain, ordinary twelve-year-old kid. Scared of my own shadow. Bite my fingernails and cry a lot. Hard to see how I can hang on here myself, let alone hide Snake Dancer . . . but I'm going to do it.

Well—first things first. She grunted as she started to gather all her gear together for the return trip to the shelter. It took about ten seconds to realize that she couldn't possibly lug that jumble of stuff back up the mountain.

After a few minutes' struggle it occurred to her to organize it better. She laid one sheet of plastic on the ground and then rolled the other plastic sheet, the blankets, and the duffel into a bundle and tied it with her belt. The food supplies were already in the knapsack. It was heavy but not impossible, she thought, as she slid her arms into the shoulder straps of the knapsack, picked up the blanket roll, and started up the steep trail.

Halfway up—and an hour later—she decided that it *was* impossible, a dead weight, and that she would make medical history by being the youngest person ever to die of a heart attack. Only trouble was that no one would ever know what happened because they would never find her corpse here on this torturous trail. She let the bundle fall, eased off the knapsack, and then collapsed beside them, with her chest heaving and sweat rolling down inside her clothes. It must be near noon, she thought, staring dizzily at the shadows of the pine trees on the steep slope. Noon, and I'm hungry and thirsty and tired, and I don't know if I can make it all the way to the top. Got to rest. She closed her eyes and lay back against a tree beside the trail, listening to the humming of some bugs in the grass nearby.

Minutes passed and the ache in her legs died away. A slight breeze was blowing up the ridge and it felt cool on her hot face. Come to think of it—it felt too cool. Solveig sat up and looked around.

Far across the valley to the south an enormous bank of clouds had appeared out of nowhere, towering high into the sky. Their tops were as white as whipped cream, fading to pearl gray halfway down, and their bases were a still, velvety black.

Oh, wow. Solveig scrambled to her feet and shouldered the pack. A storm. That's all I need—to get caught out in the rain. I've got to get up to the shelter—

She had to rest a dozen times before the upper end of the trail came in sight, and another hour or more passed in the struggle. The clouds surged higher and higher and by the time she dragged one weary foot after the other past the lookout point, the sun had vanished and a cold wind was whipping through the trees.

She was close to being too tired to care, but—yes—Snake Dancer was still there where she had left him.

Well, *almost*.

Solveig halted, peering through strands of sweaty hair that had fallen over her face. What were those strange yellowish lines that surrounded the horse, and why was he standing at such an odd angle, his head snubbed almost to the ground and one foot up?

Oh, wow. The rope.

Snake Dancer had sewed himself up in his rope like a spider spinning a web, only *he* was the one trapped in it, instead of a fly. Solveig dropped the pack and plodded wearily across the clearing, taking in details as she went. Snake Dancer had eaten the grass, the hay, and the twigs off all the bushes he could reach, and then pawed the ground till he was standing in a shallow hole. Then, for want of other entertainment, he had started playing thread-the-needle with his rope and the trees around him. Now his eyes were bulging, and in the struggle to free himself he had gotten one bad rope burn, would soon have several more.

I think I'm going to cry, she said to herself. No, I can't cry now. Get him out first. *Then* cry. She waded into the ankle-deep dust and started trying to unwind the horse. Releasing his foot was easy, as he only had one loop of rope around it. But then it was a matter of leading him back around the same tree two or three times, in and out, and watching to see that the rope was not crossing itself up again. Snake Dancer, once his foot was free and his head up again, quickly reasserted his right to take charge of his own destiny, and he was unable to see the need for passing *under* the rope this time and *over* it the next time. Before the last knot was unraveled, he balked. Knowing his mood (disgust) and the likelihood (strong) of his running away, she was afraid to simply untie the rope. So she braced her feet and pulled forward. Snake Dancer braced his legs and pulled back. Her feet slipped in the dust and Solveig went down on her back with a crash.

I am. I *am* going to cry. Solveig rolled over, laid her face on one arm, and started to sob. She was exhausted, sweaty, thirsty, scared, and a dumb horse she was trying to save from being stolen wouldn't allow himself to be led out of a trap. Why *not* cry?

For several seconds she felt enormous relief in putting all her effort into a real *bawl*. Kicked her feet. Made faces.

Then she felt something else. A soft touch, something round and padded like a hand in a boxing glove on her leg, her back, her shoulder. She rolled over and looked up. Directly above her, blotting out the sky, was Snake Dancer. Unable to bear the torment of unsatisfied curiosity (what was making that funny noise?) he had walked voluntarily out of the last knot and now stood, head down, peering into her face.

Slowly Solveig crawled to her feet. Blew her nose. Reached up for the rope. Thought that probably both of them could do with a drink of water. . . .

Snake Dancer drank till she thought he would burst, and then chewed and slobbered water over her boots. Solveig dipped up clean water in her hand, wondering if she would die of some obscure disease by drinking water with a horse. Oh, well, worry about that later.

They had no sooner finished drinking when the first drops of rain began to fall. Solveig snapped to her feet and trotted toward the shelter. Snake Dancer pounded obediently along behind her, his head weaving and his ears up as he siphoned in big draughts of cold air. Inside the shelter she tied Snake

Dancer where he wouldn't trample her pack and gave him a block of hay. He settled down to a steady crunch, crunch just as the clouds turned the faucet on and the rain began to pour down.

One last thing. She had to have another look at the camp. Leaving Snake Dancer occupied with his hay, she dashed madly down the hill to the lookout point.

Oh, wow. The van was back. So were all four of the men. Solveig watched glumly as they went into the cookhouse and shut the door. No doubt they were going to have a good hot lunch beside the big black iron stove before they started looking for Snake Dancer.

But they would probably wait till the rain stopped. So, until then—

Chapter 10

SNAKE DANCER ate most of his hay and then dropped into a doze—head drooping, eyes half closed, resting first one hind foot and then the other on the rim of the hoof. Solveig had made herself a lunch out of canned peaches and luncheon meat, and now, with her back to a bale of hay and one of the blankets pulled around her shoulders, there was nothing to do but sit and think.

The worst part of it all, she felt, was the fact that one of the bandits was Sandoz, the riding master. Sandoz, although he was old and lame and couldn't get around very well, would know all the trails in the mountains around the camp. She might give the others the slip, but Sandoz would be hard to dodge. He was there to teach the girls to know horses and to ride, and he was a good teacher—Solveig knew that without old Sandoz's instruction she would never have stayed on Snake Dancer's back during that wild runaway yesterday. And although there were only a few times she could remember seeing Sandoz *on* a horse (he had a lame leg; he was old), he could certainly ride, and ride well. With the other men pressing him to locate Snake Dancer, Solveig was sure he would do it.

Of course, there was some advantage to Solveig that Sandoz didn't know she was there. Anyway, not yet. So far as he and the others knew, they were simply trailing a horse that had managed somehow to get out of the corral. And as soon as the rain quit, they were certain to saddle up some of the other horses and start a real search. As soon as the rain stopped.

Solveig crept to the open side of the shelter and looked out. Far from quitting, the rain was falling more heavily by the minute, a powerful downpour that lashed the trees and bushes and pooled into every depression in the ground, splashed over rocks and down slopes. Luckily Solveig had never been depressed by rain or bad weather. It was exciting to watch the monstrous power of a storm, to outwit it with shades and shelters, even to plunge right into it and let it fling itself all around you while you went your way un-harmed. No, she was not afraid of the storm.

But she *was* afraid of the men who wanted Snake Dancer.

After a while she got tired of watching the rain and began to look around for something else to do. She groomed Snake Dancer thoroughly with an old currycomb she found hanging on the back wall of the shelter; then she examined his feet, checked the fit of his halter, gave him a few more bites of hay. Watching his big square teeth seize the hay made her think of teeth, toothpaste, toothbrushes, her duffel bag. A little thought clicked in the back of her mind, and she hurried over to the duffel. Under her red pajamas, hairbrush, and toilet articles was a stack of *Western Horseman* magazines. She always put a few of them in the duffel first when she was going somewhere so she would have something to read if things got dull. *Western Horseman* was a good magazine, chock-full of horse lore. If she could learn about Ruidoso anywhere, it would be in *Western Horseman.*

It took about half an hour, but she finally found it: an article on the All American Futurity. It was like the Kentucky Derby, she read, but it was for quarter horses. And it was run every year on Labor Day at Ruidoso Downs, New Mexico. The size of the purses took her breath away: value to winner (whatever that meant) was a cool $336,629.00 to Possumjet in 1972, and $330,000.00 each to Time To Thinkrich in 1973 and Easy Date in 1974. Wow! Solveig's eyes bulged. If Sandoz and the other men thought Snake Dancer could win that kind of money, they weren't going to give up trying to locate him.

Reminded now of Sandoz, she dropped the magazine. It would be a good idea to take a quick look down the mountain to see if there was any activity at the camp. She tossed a blanket over her head and raced down to the lookout point.

Her heart sank. Rain or no rain, the search was on.

Horses had been saddled and the four men were mounted. One of them—not Sandoz, probably—carried a rifle. All of them had good yellow slickers and wide-brimmed hats so they could ride comfortably through the continuing downpour.

She considered trying to stay on at the shelter, and immediately discarded the idea. It was too easy and obvious a place to search. Knowing there was hay stored there, Sandoz would be sure to check it to see if Snake Dancer might be there, rather than trying to find grass to graze on out in the forest. No—she would have to leave the shelter. But where could she go? It was impossible to take Snake Dancer down the steep trail, circle the camp to the north, and make a run for the highway, because in many places that trail consisted of steps cut into solid rock. Besides, any approach to the camp filled her with terror. No—the best plan now seemed to be to fall back into the high country and put as much distance as possible between herself and the horse thieves. If she could just hang on to Snake Dancer a little longer, someone was sure to come looking for her. She just had to hang on.

She took one blanket and wrapped the canned food in it, covered it with a plastic sheet, and tied it with a piece of rope from the shelter. The knapsack, no longer useful because she was riding instead of walking, she hid with the duffel in the bushes near the spring. Saddling and bridling Snake Dancer took a few minutes because he was restive and snorty, but she was careful to do everything right. This was no time to risk having the saddle turn on her, or a sore wear into his back to make him get cranky and pitch her off. For added safety, she left the halter on under the bridle, so she could take the bridle off to rest and graze him, and still hold him with the halter rope. When the saddle was on, she lashed the bundle behind the cantle.

After putting the blanket and the piece of plastic sheeting up on top of the stack of bales near the open side of the shelter, she led Snake Dancer out into the rain. The roof was too low for her to mount inside. The moment she was outside, the rain poured over her, streaming into her eyes and down her neck. Her feet were instantly soaked in the puddles as Snake Dancer pranced and snapped his head, and she careened wildly around, clinging to the saddle horn and yelling like an idiot before she could get herself into the saddle.

Finally up, she breathed a faint prayer of thanksgiving and urged Snake Dancer over next to the piled hay. Leaning out

58

carefully, she picked up the remaining blanket and the sheet of plastic. Snake Dancer snorted and jittered as she draped first the blanket and then the plastic around her. "Only think," she muttered, "what he would have done if I'd tried to get on him with all this stuff flapping around me! Show of the century, it would have been."

At last she was ready. With one final regretful look around at the shelter and the clearing, she sighed, sniffled, and turned Snake Dancer's head directly into the thickest, roughest part of the forest.

Well, she thought, here goes nothing.

Solveig had deliberately picked a direction where there was no trail to follow, and it only took about a minute to realize that traveling this way—breaking trail through heavy forest in a drenching rain—was going to be unbelievably hard. The rain made the footing slippery and at every step Snake Dancer's hooves slid several inches, then buried themselves and had to be pulled out of the sticky mud. Bushes reached out to scrape, trees poured water on them. Solveig shut her eyes, then opened them. She had to guide Snake Dancer or he would circle around and head for the camp where a warm dry barn awaited. She gritted her teeth and forced herself to watch ahead, behind, off to the sides.

By luck she had chosen to head off up the flank of a slope that steepened quickly and turned into a deep, brushy draw. Before long she could look across and see the opposite side of the ravine, and realized that she was climbing steadily toward the upper end of a canyon. She could no longer see the shelter or the camp, and for one panicky moment wondered what would happen if she got lost—the wild country surrounding the camp extended for miles in all directions.

But then she remembered old Sandoz's advice again, "Give your horse his head and he'll always take you home." Snake Dancer would always find his way back to the camp when she felt it was safe to go. She would simply have to keep out of sight of the men, stay ahead of them, and be ready to slip back into camp when her rescuers showed up.

For another few minutes they climbed steadily, and now the ravine was so steep and narrow that Snake Dancer could hardly keep his footing. She would have let him walk at the bottom of the cleft where there was a path of sorts (probably made by deer), but the water cascading down the steep sides had turned it into a little creek. They splashed back and forth across it several times, and each time the water seemed deeper.

Suddenly the draw ended. They had come to the head of it and were now facing a cross ridge running at right angles to the ravine. Directly in front of them was a jumble of rocks, with vines and trees growing out of crevices and draped down like waving green curtains. In several places small hollows opened under and behind the rocks, and she wished urgently that she could find one big enough for her and Snake Dancer to get into and out of the rain. But they were too shallow to afford any shelter, and she turned the horse's head to the left, urging him up the flank of the main ridge.

They climbed steadily for fifteen minutes and Solveig was beginning to wonder what she would do if Snake Dancer gave out—his flanks were heaving—when the steep pitch ended and she saw they had come up beside a high rimrock. To her left the land fell away steeply to the valley where the camp was located, and to her right the rimrock towered like an endless red wall.

Solveig's heart sank. In this country a rimrock could run for miles without a break, and it would be impossible for her to count on being able to get through it to the top of the mesa beyond, where the going would have been so much easier. Her plan, such as it was, consisted of simply staying out of sight, swinging wide around the valley, and putting herself into a position on the south side where she could slip back to the camp the moment the rescue party showed up. This meant that she would have to go west some distance, following the rimrock, before cutting south again. As she turned the horse's head and pressed her heels to his flanks, she knew the only chance they had now for shelter would be to find an overhang in the rim.

At the south end of the lake four mounted men stared bleakly across the pasture toward the dark forest. The horses snorted and splashed as they stood head to head while their riders talked.

"Most horses will run for cover in weather like this." Old Sandoz peered about him through the dripping trees. He was hunched over, riding with difficulty.

"Snake Dancer ain't like most horses. If he was, we wouldn't be lookin' for him." The speaker was a tall, heavy man with a short beard that made his face look as if it were trying to hide. His eyes and eyebrows were such a light color that he seemed not to have any at all.

"Kramer—" old Sandoz addressed the bearded man "—you know as well as I do that a horse is like any other animal. He'll look out for number one. Weather like this, he'll head for the low country."

"I don't know." Kramer's invisible eyes searched the flat lower reaches of the valley. "We covered the lower end of the valley and the meadows good this morning, and we didn't see no tracks, no hide nor hair of him. He's got to be up high."

"High or low, you better find him." Sandoz and Kramer turned to study the third man, who held a rifle under his arm, as his horse kicked sullenly and turned, trying to bite his leg. "Snake Dancer is worth a bundle and I don't aim to lose him. I didn't steal him off the Wind River Ranch and haul him all the way up here just to let a prize pair of fools like you lose him in a little rainstorm."

"Finn, nobody here has got x-ray eyes. We got to figure out where the horse is going, and then go there too."

"Why don't you track him?" The fourth man, short, fat, and blond, sat on his pony like an egg dressed up in clothes, and he rolled dangerously in the saddle every time his horse shifted. (Meg, his pony, known among the girls as Murdering Meg, for good reason, had already discovered her rider's incapacity and was planning diversions in his honor.) Sandoz, with icy contempt, had dubbed the fat man Dumpling and considered him the weakest member of their team.

All three men stared at the egg-shaped man in disgust.

"Track a horse in this rain?" Sandoz spat into a puddle. "Turn around, Bauman. You see any tracks behind *us*?"

Bauman stared glumly over his shoulder at the trail down which they had just ridden. In the driving rain every hoof-print looked like every other—although they had come down it only a few minutes ago, it was already getting hard to tell the freshest marks from the old ones.

"No." Sandoz pulled his hat down over his eyes. "We wanta find that horse, we got to do it the hard way. Separate. Make a big sweep. Take all afternoon, but one of us is bound to spot him. He'll have a halter on and each of us has got a rope. Whoever sees him, gonna have to get a rope on him. But whatever you do—don't spook him. You got to come up to him easy and gentle. Because once he starts running, there ain't anybody—or any horse—can catch him. Let's get started."

Sandoz turned sharply to the left and kicked his gelding in the flanks. In a few seconds he had vanished into the trees. After a moment the others moved out, each in a different direction.

Chapter 11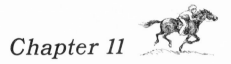

SOLVEIG guessed that it must be about four or five o'clock. Her watch had stopped because she had forgotten to wind it, but the slowly fading light gave her a late-afternoon feeling. On the off chance that she was guessing right, she set the hands of the watch at four-thirty and wound it. From time to time the rain shifted in value—heavy to light and back to heavy again—but never stopped. The ground slanted steeply away so the water ran off quickly, but the broken boulders scattered along the base of the rim made it necessary to zigzag back and forth.

After following the rim for half an hour in a westerly direction, Solveig pulled Snake Dancer's head around and faced him into a small brushy arroyo that cut down from the edge of the mesa. There was a slight overhang here, the first she had been able to find, and some protection from the wind. Best of all, there was a little swale where a patch of grass grew, and she could put a rope on Snake Dancer's halter, take off his bridle, and let him feed.

She dismounted, listening to her knees creak; she was already stiff with the cold. Taking the saddle and blanket off, she stuffed them way back under the rock where they would be out of the rain. Tying a knot in the very end of Snake Dancer's rope (to give a little added safety if he should start to jerk it out of her hand), she could let him graze while she herself was out of the rain.

Solveig crouched close under the rock, her knees up, staring out at Snake Dancer, the dripping forest, the gathering dusk. "A horse. Here I am on this lousy mountain, in this rotten rain, and all for the want—" she smiled grimly at the pun "—all for the want of a horse. In the beginning I just wanted to ride him, and then when I found out someone was going to steal him, I wanted to keep him safe.

"Why? What is so important about a *horse*? For two years I've spent almost all of my allowance helping to pay for Jubilee's board at the farm, and every girl I know envies me. *Why*?

"A horse is just a dumb, four-legged animal, head on one end, tail on the other. In between a back to ride on. You ride a horse to get from here to there, like a bus, or a car, or a bicycle. Bridle him—if you can!—put on a saddle, crack the whip. Head comes up, tail switches, hooves clatter over the ground. In the old days, used to fight wars, or herd cattle, or pull the plow and wagon. Sometimes they follow hounds, other times a hearse with empty boots in the stirrups. Eats hay, needs a stable, a pasture, has to be shod—and all of this just for the pleasure of his company.

"Lord, what *is* there about a horse? A horse will kick you, bite you, throw you off and run away, but you'll always catch him, pick up the reins, and climb on him again. A bicycle is just a bicycle, but a horse is a HORSE. . . ."

65

Solveig dozed for a few minutes with her head down on her knees. She tried not to think about things like raincoats, mothers and fathers, dry clothes, policemen, hot chocolate with marshmallows, or penicillin shots. Instead, with her eyes closed, she forced herself to confront some other salient points: 1) she and Snake Dancer were miles from any shelter in a bad storm; 2) they would surely have to spend another night in the wilderness; 3) they were lost, a fact of no apparent concern to anyone except Solveig; and 4) they were the object of a vigorous search by four men who could—and almost certainly would—do them harm if and when they caught up with them.

There was one tiny thought floating around in the back of her mind like a wood chip in a tumbling stream. It was only one item, but it might make a big difference—it might make all the difference—when the whole crazy mess sorted itself out. She was certain that the men did not know she was with Snake Dancer.

She had been very careful to cover her tracks, leave no sign of her presence anywhere about the camp or the shelter, and as the search party she had expected since yesterday had not yet appeared, the horse thieves had no way of knowing Solveig was there. They would think that they were simply tracking a runaway horse, a horse that would stop to feed, travel slowly, straying here and there as his fancy called, riderless and undirected.

Actually they were on the trail of a team—a very fast horse and a grimly determined girl—and sooner or later a rescue party was going to show up looking for Solveig. *Weren't they?* And with these two surprises up her sleeve, Solveig hoped she could play out her part in the affair reasonably well.

She was cold and stiff from sitting still so long. Time to move on. She sighed, stretched, raised her head.

"Hey! What? My horse. He's gone!"

Actually, he wasn't gone.

He had just turned into a different horse. Snake Dancer— a deep, sable-brown horse with a sable-brown mane and tail —had turned, while she was resting her head on her knees, into a strange, splotchy animal with a splotchy gray back, head, and rump, and a brown belly and legs. His mane and tail were neither color but something in between.

Solveig scrambled to her feet. Still holding tight to the rope, she slithered down the bank, reached out a hand, and ran it over Snake Dancer's flank. Drawing it back, she looked down. It was streaked with a deep blackish-brown substance that washed away with the rain while she was standing there look-ing at it.

Dye. Snake Dancer had been given some kind of dye job to change his color while he was to be hidden out here at Camp Ahwanee. And the steady driving rain was washing it off. His true color, now emerging, was a deep crystalline gray with white dapples like bubbles on dark water. His mane and tail were light gray, or would be when the rest of the dye was gone—closer, perhaps, to silver. All four legs and his muzzle were turning to a deep gray-black, streaked here and there with a few white hairs.

So now—she had to laugh, although things weren't all that funny—Snake Dancer was a horse of a different color.

Solveig pulled the saddle and blanket out from under the sheltering rock. As she put them on him Snake Dancer snorted, grunted, and sucked in air. His head swiveled around and he stared at her with his enormous onyx eyes shaded by sultry, inch-long lashes. His upper lip twitched back and a row of strong yellow teeth grazed her elbow. Solveig shrieked and whacked at him. "Cut it out, you *plug!*" she shouted as she leaped out of reach. Snake Dancer blinked at her with a would-*I*-do-*that*? expression. Solveig wobbled back and looked at the cinch. It looked like a string tied around a balloon. Holy torpedo juice. "Cut that *out!*" she screamed, kicking the horse in the belly. Snake Dancer, coughed, exhaled, and the cinch loosened so much it swung under his belly like a hammock. "Nice try," said Solveig grimly as she tightened it again. "If they'd had horses like you on the Ponderosa or High Chaparral, the bad guys would have wiped them out."

Snake Dancer had evidently postponed the next game due to rain and she got the bridle on without a fight. She left the halter on under it to make it easier to control him later when she would have to tether him again. Rolling up the rope, she tied it to the saddle with a latigo strap. Her foot in the stirrup touched off a few kicks and plunges, but either Solveig was getting nervier (not likely) or Snake Dancer was developing compassion (hard to believe), because in a moment or two she was up, her makeshift slicker in place.

She turned the horse's head westward down the wall of the rimrock. There was only a little daylight left and they had to find a place where they could both get in out of the storm. There had to be a place—

Chapter 12

SOLVEIG had thought the rain might lessen as darkness fell, but if anything it got harder. Snake Dancer was tired and stumbling at every other step, and they had covered very little distance by the time she decided they had to stop or run the risk of killing themselves.

Ahead on her right the bold outline of the rimrock stretched away into the night. But now there was a change in it. Squinting, she could just make out a deep overhang in the wall. Solveig kicked Snake Dancer's flank and urged him along the rock-strewn slope.

The shelf of rock was like a porch roof over them as Snake Dancer scrambled up the last little pitch. Solveig gasped as they came in out of the rain. Snake Dancer stood for a moment, flanks heaving, and then dropped his head and sniffed the ground. He did not seem to take alarm at the sight or smell of the place, and since it was too dark for her to see much, Solveig knew she would have to rely on his instincts to sense danger.

Wearily she dismounted. Taking the saddle and bridle off, she carried them farther up under the rock and laid them where it was clean and dry. The ground was fairly level here, except for a few sizable clumps of rock, and there were some old logs scattered around, probably brought in by someone who intended to use them for firewood. She tied Snake Dancer's rope to one of the logs and then sat down beside him. Her head was spinning and every bone and muscle was shrieking for rest and warmth. Snake Dancer sighed, coughed, sneezed—letting the air rattle out through loose, flapping lips. He put his head down and sniffed the ground again, snorting and blowing up great clouds of dust. It was so dark now that she could hardly see him there, an arm's length away from her, but from the sounds he was making he seemed relaxed and comfortable.

If only *I* was relaxed and comfortable. Solveig shivered as she tried to peer around her. For a long time her only thought had been to get out of the rain; now that she had found shelter, she discovered a dozen other things that clamored for attention. She was chilled to the bone; her head, neck, and shoulders were wet where the makeshift poncho kept blowing off. Her feet were icy, she was saddle-sore and starved.

Solveig tried to make herself think it all through. How dangerous would a small fire be? The shelf of rock was very deep and she was reasonably sure she could build a tiny blaze far enough back under it so it could not be seen from the outside. There were jumbled boulders scattered about the entrance that should offer a good screen, and quite a bit of dry wood, sticks and twigs, lying about on the ground. And she had matches—

Suddenly the need for warmth and light overcame everything else. With that immense attack force—black night and punishing storm—thundering out there, she had to have a fire.

By feel alone she gathered dry wisps of grass and sticks and assembled them behind the largest cluster of rocks. She put her pack nearby for the moment, and then draped the blanket she had used for a poncho over a log to dry as much as it would (and also to cut off light). Then she struck a match.

She had been afraid it wouldn't burn, but for once she was lucky. The dry grass caught quickly, then the shredded bark and twigs. In a few moments a tiny fire was crackling in a nest of small stones, and the sight, sound, smell of it were so wonderful Solveig wondered how she had stood the darkness so long. Knowing she could not risk a big fire, or let it burn very long, she quickly took her bearings. Yes—here, where it was flat and smooth, she would sleep. Over there she would lay her pack. At the edge of the rock roof was a beautiful sight— a patch of short, dry grass. The wind must have blown the seeds in under the overhang, where they sprouted and grew, though poorly, in the brief hours of sunlight that crept in during the early mornings and late evenings. Hurriedly she untied Snake Dancer and led him around to the grass and tied him up again with a safe bowline knot. "Lucky I learned to tie good knots," she grunted. "Old Sandoz taught me how to do that."

Thinking about Sandoz, and his old brown fingers that looked like the rope he handled every day, made her think of the four men on her trail—on Snake Dancer's trail. As she opened her pack and began to fix herself a meal, she wondered how long she could hold out.

Maybe one more day. Two at the most. She had enough food for tonight and tomorrow, possibly one meal on the following day. If she could keep the one blanket dry that she was using to sleep in, and the matches, that would help.

Then there was Snake Dancer. She had to be sure he had plenty of feed. Water was no problem—they were surrounded by water. Every arroyo, every hollow was running full of water, and although it was muddy and full of trash, he could drink it if he had to. And he was tough—she could only hope he was tough enough to stand the hard traveling and exposure.

But how about Solveig herself? Wolfing down the scanty supper she had allowed herself, Solveig wondered how long *she* could last. I'm tired and cold—lucky if I don't come down with the flu. It's a good thing I'm healthy. Otherwise I couldn't have made it this far.

With the fire dying, Solveig leaned back against the rock and soaked up all the heat she could, knowing she had better not risk letting it burn much longer. As the little red blaze dwindled, several lumpy thoughts continued to thump around in her head. I shouldn't have tried to do this; I should have just turned Snake Dancer loose and let them catch him; I could have kept out of sight, hung out around the camp. Then, when they were gone, all I'd have had to do would be just sit there safe and sound, out of the rain, and wait for Miss P to come back and get me.

Why didn't I do that? Who do I think I am, the hero of an adventure movie? I'm not smart or brave. I'm dumb and awkward. I thought I knew a lot about horses. And I do. But it wasn't enough. I wish I'd never tried to ride Snake Dancer. I wish I'd never gotten off the bus. I wish I was home in bed, or at school. She pictured her room at home, with its striped wallpaper, its French provincial furnishings, the soft blue rug, the windows overlooking her mother's garden. Or the dorm at school: three narrow beds to a room, crisp white sheets and matching blankets with the school crest, girls giggling and scuffling after lights-out, in spite of dark threats from the housemother.

At last the fire went out, and with it the last remnants of her courage. I'd run away, she told herself, but I've already done that, and how can you run away from running away?

In black darkness, with her ears full of the sound of the relentless rain gushing down outside, she rolled up in the dry blanket, put her head on her bent arm, and closed her eyes. Her last thought before sleep overcame her was: a learning experience. That's what Miss P said this trip to Camp Ahwanee would be, a learning experience. And, boy, has it ever been. So far I've learned that you shouldn't run away from school in the middle of a typhoon, or use washable dye when you try to change a horse's color. I'll probably learn even more tomorrow—

Chapter 13

IT WAS HARD to tell when morning came. For a long time the night was utterly black and cold, and all she could hear were the steady pounding of the rain outside the overhang and Snake Dancer's quiet noises—a sneeze, a snuffle, the thump of his hooves as he changed position, the steady *whisk, whisk* of his never-still tail. Snake Dancer's tail was like a ground wire—through it he seemed to emit excess energy that might otherwise overload his circuits and short out. Solveig amused herself briefly by imagining Snake Dancer—tail caught in a barn door, perhaps, and thus immobilized—with sparks shooting off his ears and bolts of lightning stabbing out of his onyx eyes. Like to see the horse thieves lay a hand on him *then*, she thought sourly.

Presently the blackness began to lighten to a deep gray that slowly paled to a watery, colorless light, and she could pick out a rock, a log, the tip of the tallest tree downslope from the cave. For a while, huddled in her blanket, she thought about the strange circumstance of Snake Dancer's change of color. Sandoz and the others, having hit on the idea of hiding the horse under a coat of dye so he wouldn't be recognized, would now be looking for a sable-brown horse—they wouldn't know that the dye had washed off. That might give her a very slight advantage. If they should catch a glimpse of Snake Dancer, it would be a second or two longer before they recognized him, and with a horse as fast as Snake Dancer, a few seconds could make a big difference. One thing she was sure of—as long as she stayed on reasonably solid ground, there was no way the others could run her down. They were mounted on the camp's other horses, all scrubs compared to Snake Dancer. Snake Dancer could leave them all behind as if they were standing still. The only way he could be caught would be if he were cornered where he couldn't run.

When daylight finally came, Solveig forced herself to crawl out from under the blanket. She decided against making another fire, although she would have given almost anything to warm herself over a crackling blaze. With the dry blanket over her shoulders, she finished a can of peaches she had started last night and several greasy slices of luncheon meat. I never thought I'd get tired of peaches, she thought grimly, but I'm getting there.

When she had eaten, she lashed the pack together and checked over the saddle and bridle. Then she tried to destroy any sign that a girl and a horse had found shelter for the night under the rim. Her own tracks were everywhere, and Snake Dancer's restless pawing had, as usual, left a crater where he had been tied. She took a bunch of twigs and, using it like a broom, swept away as much as she could. Snake Dancer's tracks were hard to cover, and she finally had to toss a lot of loose rocks over the spot where he had stood. With a handy stick she practiced her golf swing, lobbing balls of horse manure out from under the rimrock to land and roll down the slope. Any one of them could have been a hole-in-one, given the right tools, she thought with satisfaction.

It was full daylight now, and she had a powerful feeling that they must get moving. After saddling and bridling Snake Dancer, with the reins tied over a fallen log, Solveig went to the opening and cautiously looked out from under the rock. She hated to leave this shelter and plunge out into the rain again, and she toyed briefly with the idea of staying here, in the hope that rescuers would find her.

No chance. Dumb idea. When they came—and she was now convinced that a search party would arrive today for sure at the camp headquarters—they would have no way of locating her if she was knocking around out in the wilderness. Oh, eventually they would, but by that time she and probably Snake Dancer too would be nothing but a pile of bleached bones. (Not to mention the fact that the horse thieves would be between Solveig and the rescue party, and would be sure to throw out whatever hindrance they could, if only to clear the way for their own project.)

No, she had to get back to the camp—or near it—if she wanted to be rescued. And I *do*, I *do*. Nothing was clearer in her mind now than the fact that the next time adventure came her way, Solveig would not volunteer. No more. I've learned my lesson. If somebody sends me a mysterious tape through the mail that says, "Your mission, should you choose to accept it, is—" I'll drop it into the nearest KEEP YOUR CITY CLEAN barrel. From now on, you won't find me doing anything riskier than crossing the street with the green but DON'T WALK light. All I want is just to get out of this mess.

After lashing the pack behind the saddle, Solveig led Snake Dancer out from under the rock and mounted. She had to carry the plastic sheet and poncho over her arm and it was hard to mount with them flapping in the wind. Snake Dancer narrowly missed stepping on her foot as she danced beside him, left foot in the stirrup and the other bouncing off the ground like a pogo stick. At last she was up, the poncho over her, and she gathered up the reins.

Once she was mounted and out of the shelter of the overhang, she felt exposed as a bug on a kitchen floor. Which way to go? Quickly she turned the horse downslope into the trees. It was time to cut away from the rimrock and circle around to the south. That would take her down onto the more level land on the west side of the lake. With care she should be able to cross the open, rocky flat, swing around south of the camp, and cut through the forest to the road leading out to the highway. The road was the only way into the camp and any-one coming in—hopefully to look for her—would have to come that way. The more she thought about it, the better this idea appealed to her. It's what I would have done yesterday, she thought, but then of course it got dark and we had to camp here under the rimrock.

As she rode she kept a very sharp watch for any sign of the four men. It was hard to decide where she would be safer—at the bottom of the draws where clumps of trees and deer brush offered a good cover, or high on the ridges. They would be less visible in the draws, but it would be much harder to get away if one of the searchers caught sight of her. She decided to keep just under the crest of each ridge, so as not to be seen against the skyline, and to keep among thick trees as much as possible.

As the day wore on, it became very apparent to her that she now had to make allowances for another element. For almost eighteen hours now the rain had continued to pour with only a few minutes now and then when it lightened. The ground was saturated. In addition to struggling with the greasy mud, there was now the problem of the gullies. Early in the morning, when they started, each ravine had had a small brook running in its depths. By noon, when they were not more than halfway down from the rimrock, the brooks had become tumbling, cream-colored torrents that came above Snake Dancer's knees as he splashed through them.

Around the middle of the day she decided to call a halt. She needed food. Snake Dancer was hungry too. He had been nipping sideways at clumps of grass all morning, and they both had to have some rest. She finally located a good spot— a particularly heavy stand of trees beside a small meadow. Beyond, the ground fell away into the more open rocky flat and she needed some time to think about whether to risk crossing it, or if she should concentrate more on keeping out of sight by going farther west through the forest.

Solveig decided to unsaddle Snake Dancer, to avoid any possibility of saddle sores developing, and put the saddle and bridle under a thick spruce to keep them fairly dry. Tying the horse to a low stump, she quickly opened her pack and fixed a skimpy lunch. Then she led Snake Dancer to the grass and let him eat. He was hungry; he lost no time in stowing away a good meal.

Seated on a rock, with Snake Dancer's rope in her hand, Solveig considered her next move. She could either swing far to the west, keeping in the cover of the trees, or take a chance and go directly south, crossing an open stretch covered with a few twisted trees and a wild jumble of gray, lichened rocks. Going west would take all afternoon and it would be dark long before she would come around past the camp to the road.

On the other hand, it wouldn't take an hour to cross the rocky stretch. She was still confident that Snake Dancer could out-run any other horse that tried to catch him, especially if he weren't exhausted by extra hours of struggling through the mud. And when the rescue party came, Solveig planned to be there to welcome them with open arms.

So. It would have to be the rocky flat.

Solveig sighed. Time to get started. She slid off the rock and her feet hit the ground with a queer, splashy sound.

Snake Dancer's head snapped up. Before Solveig could blink, the rope slipped through her fingers.

Oh, Lord.

The end of the rope lay in the mud a few feet away, then began to twitch as Snake Dancer, snorting, backed away. "Whoa, whoa, boy." She stepped cautiously forward, knelt, put out her hand. But before she could grab the rope Snake Dancer yanked back a few more steps. He looked wildly around, trying to see what had made the strange noise. Solveig moved forward, talking quietly, praying urgently. Snake Dancer's head was weaving like a loaf of bread stuck on the end of a fishing rod; he moved just fast enough to stay out of her grasp. Across to the big dead pine tree. Around the clump of bushes. Back to where they started. Snake Dancer just out of reach. Solveig trembling, sweating in the cold air, always a second too late, inches short, of grabbing the rope.

Maybe play it cool? Solveig forced herself to look away, pretend to walk over to look at a certain stone near where the end of the rope lay. Snake Dancer watched her with interest, even inspected the same rock from a safe distance; it almost worked. But as her hand reached out, he backed off again.

How about chasing him? She leaped up and bolted after him. And found herself pitted against one of the world's

fastest horses. Snake Dancer was a hundred yards away while she was still plowing through the first five or ten yards of mud. Snake Dancer halted again, looking back at her, ears up. He nickered.

Solveig stood in the deep wet grass staring at Snake Dancer. What'll I do? I can't catch him. Now I'm afoot. Now I'm really lost. There's no way on earth I can get out of this mess by myself.

Her knees folded and she sank down to crouch heedlessly in the mud. She pulled the edge of the blanket over her head and began to cry. With her face on her knees she rocked back and forth, bellowing as loud as she could. Why be quiet now? Why try to hide? The game was over, lost—

She rocked and howled, beating her fists on her shins. All the sound reverberated under the blanket with her, and it flashed across her mind once that she must be making quite a spectacle—a shapeless lump under a gray blanket, thrashing around and emitting horrible noises.

A soft, rubbery object thumped her on the head. Another thump on her shoulder. Solveig, still rocking and wailing, opened her eyes.

A slit of light at the bottom of the blanket showed an interesting sight: the edge of a horse's hoof.

Solveig rocked back and forth and made more noises—strange noises. The hoof came closer, and now she could see another hoof, a deep gray leg, a piece of muddy rope. She continued to bawl and snuffle. If that's the kind of music he liked, she would serenade Snake Dancer all day.

Solveig stole a quick glance out from behind the blanket and found herself staring directly into a long-lashed, round onyx eye: Snake Dancer, overcome by curiosity, had returned and was trying to peer under the blanket to find out what was making all those funny noises.

Rocking, bellowing, Solveig put out her hand. As her fingers closed over the rope she straightened up slowly.

Snake Dancer's eyes rolled. His head snapped up, but Solveig had the rope wrapped around her wrist, and would have held on if he had dragged her across a bramble patch.

"Satisfaction killed the cat!" she screamed, kicking Snake Dancer in the belly, "but curiosity brought him back!"

Coming down out of the trees gave her an intense feeling of being exposed, in danger. Solveig kept a sharp lookout all around, but they were about halfway across the flat before anything happened to alert her to the presence of one of the horse thieves. She was jolting along, picking out an easy path and watching how Snake Dancer's strange, mottled gray-and-white coat blended so well with the gray-and-white mottled rocks, when a rifle shot rang out.

Solveig jerked Snake Dancer to a halt.

The sound came from behind her and to the west. A signal?

Another shot—this time to the south, from somewhere beyond the rocky flat. So, they had more than one gun. She decided they must be using gun shots to keep in touch as they pressed forward in a broad sweep.

Solveig slid slowly out of the saddle and stood searching the edge of the forest. She could see nothing—no one—but she knew she was now between two of the searchers. Had they seen her? Were they signaling each other to close in?

As she squinted her eyes and peered out from under Snake Dancer's neck, a brief flicker of movement far off caught her attention. There, straight west, just this side of the edge of the forest. It was a rider. At this distance she couldn't tell which man it might be. He was making his way north along the edge of the rocks and appeared to be leading another horse. "Nuts," she muttered. "They're leading extra horses to change to when the ones they're riding get tired."

She had just decided that the distant rider was no threat, when suddenly another sound made her freeze. There was a rattle of scattered rocks and the soft thump of a horse's hooves, and it sounded as loud as if it were inside her head. Snake Dancer's ears picked up and she barely had time to leap to his head and grab his muzzle to keep him from whinnying. There was just a moment to whirl him around behind a clump of rocks and yank his head down before the rider—it was the man Sandoz called Dumpling—bobbed into sight.

Solveig held her breath. Would the rider see them? Part of Snake Dancer's broad rear was sticking out from behind the inadequate cover. Snake Dancer grunted, threatening to hoist her off the ground, but she held him as still as the mottled gray rocks around him.

It almost worked. The man looked directly at Snake Dancer's square, heavy rump—speckled and spotted in shades of gray—and came close to taking it for just another lichened rock. But then Snake Dancer flicked his tail and the game was up. Solveig threw the reins up over Snake Dancer's head, leaped into the saddle, and bending low over his neck, dug her heels into the horse's sides. Snake Dancer took off from a standing start as if he were breaking out of a starting gate at the race track.

For a moment Solveig could only think of the loose rocks, the broken trees underfoot, the sticky mud. She was aware of the horse's hooves striking the ground like hammers, the enormous power of his body stretching and contracting for each stride as the ground fell away behind them. There was a sudden squall of rain that she would have cursed if she had had time or breath.

But when she snatched a look back over her shoulder she could see the fat man—nearsighted, puzzled, a misfit in this game of cat and mouse—shake his head and turn his horse away. He had been told to watch for a sable-brown horse, a horse that would stand out against the gray rocks like a lighthouse on a stormy coast. The horse he had barely glimpsed rocketing away in the mist was not the one he had been looking for. Sandoz and Kramer would have recognized Snake Dancer in a moment, but the Dumpling's untrained eye—and Snake Dancer's matchless strength and speed—had saved them.

On the far side of the rocky stretch and well into the safety of the trees, Solveig pulled Snake Dancer up. He slithered reluctantly to a halt and stood, barely winded, as she turned to search the open flat for signs of her followers. She sighed shakily as she rubbed her hand over Snake Dancer's neck. Stars and Garters! What a horse. What a *horse*.

Chapter 14

CROSSING the rocks had saved her a lot of time. It was about midafternoon when she drew abreast of the lake and then passed around the south end of the pasture, keeping always in the trees. She was sure that two of the men were behind her, but that left two more who could be anywhere. Her neck was getting sore from constantly swiveling her head around to watch in all directions. So far, so good. She had seen *them,* but as nearly as she could tell, from the very start the thieves had never laid eyes on her or the horse, not counting the fat man on Meg, who hadn't recognized Snake Dancer.

It was probably somewhere near five o'clock, the light waning, the rain still heavy, when Solveig crossed south of the camp itself. The trees here had thinned and she had to detour quite a' distance to avoid being seen. It was possible that one man might have been stationed at the camp for any of several reasons, and she wanted to be sure he didn't see her.

Her plan was to circle around and come out near the road that led to the highway. Then she would cross the bridge and follow the road (keeping hidden among the trees) until she came to the highway, where there were a few scattered ranches to which she could go for help. Or it might be that she would meet someone coming up the road to look for her. She no longer expected to see the big yellow bus, of course, but there would likely be cars—her parents', Miss P's, maybe the county sheriff's. Anything. Anybody. Lord, she prayed, just send me somebody to help me get out of this. I can't hold on much longer.

She wondered at times why she didn't just give up, let the men overtake her and capture Snake Dancer. I'm not really brave, not a real crime fighter. The more she thought about her original impulse—jumping off the bus, snatching one quick forbidden ride on the horse that had been denied her—she realized that it had all been false. *I* knew I could ride Snake Dancer, and I should have been satisfied with that. I'm luckier than most kids. I have a horse of my own. But, no, I had to go one step further and prove how smart I was to everyone else.

And then—and then I found out how great Snake Dancer was, and I couldn't let him go. The kind of people who would steal a horse in the first place would run him till he dropped. And there ought to be something better for him than that. I know he can't be mine, but at least I can try to hang on long enough to get him back to his real owners. Snake Dancer is a horse for X. Y. Z. I only wish *I* was X. Y. Z.

As she passed the camp, Snake Dancer began to bear left, trying to make his way back to the corral and the stable. There were no lights anywhere, but some of the horses stood in the corral. Snake Dancer's head swung around as if attracted by a magnet, and it took all of Solveig's strength to yank him back into the trees. Whenever he came to an obstacle—tree, rock, or bush—he insisted on going to the left as if the right side were impassable. When she pulled him to the right, he stumbled and blundered because he was looking back over his shoulder. Once or twice he stopped completely, and Solveig had to slap him again and again with the ends of the reins to get him started.

Finally the camp was behind them. Snake Dancer plodded forward, his head swinging as he watched the darkening forest. Presently his ears began to funnel forward, twitch back, then forward again. Before long he halted again, put his head down, and sniffed the ground.

Solveig groaned. At this rate they would never get away from the camp, much less far enough down the road to be safe. The ground here sloped somewhat toward the river, and the cover of trees was thin. Patches of water lay here and there, and more time was lost because Snake Dancer insisted on walking around them instead of splashing through. But she realized, of course, that he was bone-tired from fighting the sticky mud all day.

Even more unsettling than the wet ground was the soft, creepy sound that she could now hear. Snake Dancer had been hearing it for some time, and now would only go forward a few feet at a time, then stop, listen, then forward a few more steps. It was not quite a rumble that she heard, but it sounded like—

Oh, Lord. A *flood*. The river was in flood.

Solveig jerked Snake Dancer to a halt, staring in disbelief. The river was over its banks. And over the bridge. She could not even see the bridge—it was under several feet of thundering water, thick and wild, full of fallen trees and brush. The water swept past her like the flood in the Book of Genesis.

And I haven't got an Ark.

Well, now I know why nobody has come after me. They can't get across the river. Nobody can get up that road now. It would take an airplane to get in here, and an airplane couldn't land—the only clear places are all too small. So I'm penned in behind a flood with a bunch of guys who are out to steal a valuable horse and if they catch up with me (her heart sank), they'll just pitch me into that river. Everyone, mom and dad, Miss P—will think I slipped and fell in, trying to get across and make it back home after I got left here. Because one kid more or less isn't going to matter to Sandoz and Kramer.

There was no longer any point in trying to go forward. And as she swung Snake Dancer back away from the river, she had reached the point where she was too tired to think.

Snake Dancer, given his head at last, after two days of bending (more or less) to the will of his rider, turned and started for home—the warm, dry stable where he knew he would find feed and clean water, and relief from the lonely, threatening forest, the endless struggle with the mud. There would be other horses there, and the easy stamping, shoulder-rubbing, tail-whisking commerce of his own kind.

Solveig rode, swaying in the saddle, trying to force herself to brace up, wondering hazily what to do now. Before she realized it, they had left the cover of the trees. Snake Dancer had zeroed in on the stable; his gait freshened and his head was up, ears twitching forward. The corral was dead ahead —across from the loading zone—and beside it the figures of four men on horseback.

In one disastrous flash Solveig saw that they had blundered

into full sight of the horse thieves, who had the awful luck to be in a cluster right by the stable. Mounted. Ready to ride.

Solveig whirled Snake Dancer and clamped her heels into his sides. Snake Dancer squealed and reared. Then, stretching out, belly down, he started to run. And even on the muddy ground, tired as he was, they would never have caught him—

—if there had been any place to run *to*—

Even before the clear ground ended, and long before the pursuers had closed the gap, she knew it was hopeless. The river—the flood—they had been trapped in the only flat open space they had crossed in two days. It was all over now.

Wearily she pulled Snake Dancer up. No use squandering his last bit of strength. Great, gallant Snake Dancer at least should be saved—to run again. It was his life—his soul—and he must be saved to run again.

If only her head didn't hurt so—roaring and rattling like an immense engine. The vibrations of it stunned her.

Now she sat waiting for the men as they came pounding on.

But—that *noise*? She looked up.

Oh, Lord. *Helicopters.*

She couldn't believe it. No. Things like that happened in movies. On TV.

Yes. Helicopters!

Snake Dancer reared up screaming and started to bolt as the grotesque bawling birds settled down on either side of him. Then he saw the edge of the water. He slammed to a halt and whirled.

Turn—on—a—nickel—was the last thing Solveig thought of as she hit the soggy ground.

Chapter 15

COLD, GRITTY WATER splashed in her face. Solveig blacked out for a second, then automatically rolled over, trying to get out from under Snake Dancer's flying hooves. It flashed through her mind that she had spent a lot of time lately escaping from those murderous pile drivers.

Her head was pounding as she sat up in the awful sticky mud. She stared up at Snake Dancer, who was snorting and pitching, lashing out at a couple of strange men who had appeared out of nowhere and were trying to catch him.

Some lady was trying to grab her, but Solveig pushed her away and wobbled to her feet. "Hey—Snake Dancer—don't you guys *hurt* that horse."

"Hurt—*him*?" screamed one of the men as Snake Dancer's teeth grazed his shoulder and ripped the sleeve off his coat. Odd, thought Solveig hazily, the fellow seemed to be wearing some kind of uniform. If I can just get away from this woman I'll catch Snake Dancer. There is so much *noise*—

Woman?

She looked around.

"Mom!"

"Solveig! Baby!" Her mother's face was a sweet, wonderful blur in the dusk, like an angel, like a favorite flower in the moonlight.

"Mom!" Solveig threw her arms around her mother for one great, furious hug. Then she pulled herself up. "Help me—"

"Yes, darling—"

"—catch Snake Dancer—" Still gripping her mother's hand, Solveig pushed herself over to where Snake Dancer was thundering around like a loose cannon on the deck of a ship. She reached up and laid one hand on his shoulder, unmindful of the trampling hooves, the teeth that could lay her skin open like a plow.

As she put her arm around his neck, Snake Dancer rumbled to a halt. His sides were heaving, his nostrils flared, and his sensitive ears were flat back, but he stood still for *her*. Not for the men in the uniforms, not for the man who had come from behind them—a big man in a cowboy hat. For *her*. Solveig Nilsson. Crime-fighter. Hero of the kidnapped quarter-horse caper.

"Gentle as a kitten," said Solveig, with her face plastered to Snake Dancer's sweaty shoulder.

"Sure," said Cowboy Hat.

"Sure," said Torn Sleeve. He picked at the ribbons Snake Dancer had created out of his coat.

"Sure," said Solveig's father.

"Dad." Solveig turned, still holding on to Snake Dancer. "Where did you all come from? One minute I was all alone, and they were going to catch us—me and Snake Dancer—and the next minute—" Solveig waved wildly at the crowd of people who had hatched out of the helicopters. "Wow! The Star Ship landed and here comes *everybody*!"

94

"Darling—you *knew* we'd be coming after you." Her mother had grabbed up the torn coat sleeve and was dabbing at the mud on Solveig's face. "The minute we found out you were missing at school we started to look for you! But this awful flood—we couldn't get in with cars or even trucks—this *rain!*"

"Solveig," her father leaned over. "Let the horse go now, darling. He'll be all right. Mr. Roby is a rancher. He came with the search party to help us find you, and he'll take care of the horse."

Solveig looked up at Cowboy Hat. "He's an awful good horse," she told him. "*They* were going to steal him, you know. But I wouldn't let them get him. We ran off—hid out—"

John Roby and Solveig's father exchanged glances. "No wonder the sheriff rounded them up so fast when we got out of the helicopter," said Glenn Nilsson. "That's the missing piece to the puzzle. We knew *you* must be here at camp—anyway, you weren't at the Academy and we thought you must be here—"

"And we knew a valuable horse had been stolen and was probably being hid out somewhere around here—"

"But we didn't know we'd find you together," said her mother.

"What else?" muttered Solveig Nilsson, otherwise known as Xenia Y. Zilch, heroine of who-knows-what-all capers, as she wiped her nose on the back of her hand.

Chapter 16

SOLVEIG sat huddled in a dry blanket and stared sleepily at the fire crackling in the huge stone fireplace. The camp's manager had returned with the search party to offer his assistance, and, considering the short notice, had produced satisfying refreshments. Crockery and spoons clattered, mugs clinked; there was a holiday atmosphere in the room. I haven't seen so much jollity, thought Solveig, since the Christmas party at school last year when the music teacher drank too much punch and pasted a red sequin on the end of her nose and danced around singing, "Rude-nose, the Red-olph Reindeer."

Mrs. Nilsson had helped to make a big pot of coffee on the cookstove, and now everyone was standing or sitting around in the lounge swilling up the hot coffee and all talking at once.

All except the horse thieves—Sandoz, Kramer, Finn, and the Dumpling. They sat in a silent cluster, handcuffed, waiting to be transported by helicopter to the county jail. From time to time one of them glared at her, but Solveig just returned a stony stare and sipped at the cup of coffee (half hot milk) that her mother had poured for her.

She was terribly tired but there were some things she had to straighten out before she could feel free to roll up in the blanket and go to sleep. "Dad—Mom—"

"Yes, darling?"

"It's, well—" Solveig swallowed, started over again. "It's my own dumb fault I got into this mess. It wasn't Miss P's fault I got left behind. I did it on purpose. I had this crazy thing about riding Snake Dancer. So don't blame Miss P. It was just an impulse—I jumped off the bus without thinking twice—like somebody in a book or movie having a great big adventure. I was so sure Miss P would miss me and come back. I never dreamed all this—" Solveig waved feebly at the small army of men who had been mustered to rescue her "—would happen. Then, when I found out about the guys trying to steal Snake Dancer, I thought I could keep him away from them. I didn't stop to think—I just took off with him." Solveig's nose was starting to drip again and she sneezed. Knew I would catch the flu, she thought drearily. "I'm lucky I didn't kill myself—or Snake Dancer."

The elder Nilssons stared bleakly at each other.

"One thing I couldn't figure out, Mom. How come the bus didn't come right back as soon as they saw I was missing? Miss P must have known I was gone by the time they were a mile away. I counted on her doing that, you know. I thought —Mom?"

"Darling," Mrs. Nilsson's face was grave, "Miss P is very sick."

"Sick?"

"Something like a heart attack. It happened just as the bus was leaving. In all the excitement—rushing her to the doctor and all—no one realized you were missing."

Solveig thought about Miss P soberly. "The mouse?"

They all looked puzzled.

"Somebody put a mouse in her purse. I heard her scream."

"Well, that probably upset her, but she had been ill for some time. The attack could have come any time."

Solveig blew her nose in the big clean handkerchief her father offered. At last she was fitting some missing pieces into her own puzzle. "So I went out and got myself lost and fell smack into somebody's plan to steal a horse. And just because the horse ran away with me—" several pairs of eyebrows rose quickly "—I ruined it for them."

Mr. Nilsson nodded. "We'll have a good long talk later about this business of sneaking off the bus, Solveig," he said grimly. "Do you realize what could have happened to you if the sheriff here hadn't been able to get help from the National Guard—these men with the helicopters—to come out here and look for you?"

Solveig nodded glumly. Oh, boy. Do I *ever*.

"I wonder if we'll ever know the whole story?" asked Mrs. Nilsson thoughtfully.

Jeez—I sure hope not, thought Solveig to herself as she sneezed again. There's quite a bit here I'm not too proud of . . . "How are they going to get the horses out of here now with the flood?" she asked, to change the subject.

"Oh, that's no problem," said Mr. Roby confidently. "Soon as the water goes down a couple of my ranch hands will take them out. Somebody will ride Snake Dancer and a couple of the others, and we'll lead or drive the rest."

"Ride—Snake Dancer?" Solveig bent her head so no one could see the evil smile that spread over her face. "Ah, yes. That will be a *learning experience*." She took out the handkerchief and blew her nose again. Her face was hot and her throat felt like gravel. I thought I knew something about horses from having one of my own, but I learned a *lot* more from Snake Dancer, she told herself. I learned that you shouldn't dress up like Bat Man and then try to get on a nervous horse, and that sometimes the people you thought were the good guys turn out to be the bad guys—she glanced sullenly at Sandoz—and if it rains for two days you will probably find yourself in a flood, and that a horse will buck you off if a helicopter lands right beside him.

Most of all, I learned what it takes to be X. Y. Z. And that's not bad, for a beginning.

"Take good care of him," Solveig told Mr. Roby. "Snake Dancer is some horse. He's a horse for X. Y. Z. . . ."

And she wondered, as she drifted off to sleep, why they all looked so puzzled.

LOUISE MOERI grew up on ranches in Oregon and California, and cannot remember a time when she did not have horses until she left home to go to college. Then the equine dimension dropped out of her life (but not her heart!) until her own daughter was bitten by "horse fever." Her plea to "get a horse" led the family to the half-acre place in Manteca, California, which they still have, and to a series of ponies and horses.

Having worked for over fifteen years as a library assistant, Mrs. Moeri says she knew she would be pleasing a lot of readers as well as herself and her daughter if she could write a horse story. But it took a long time, and one published book, *Star Mother's Youngest Child* (Houghton Mifflin), before this story finally came to her.

GAIL OWENS was born and raised in Detroit, Michigan. She attended a variety of art schools, and has always worked as a commercial artist—illustrator, designer, art director. She has illustrated a number of books, including *A Bedtime Story* and *The Santa Claus Mystery*, both written by Joan Goldman Levine, and *I'll Tell on You*, written by Joan Lexau. She lives in a small town in the New York countryside.

W/D

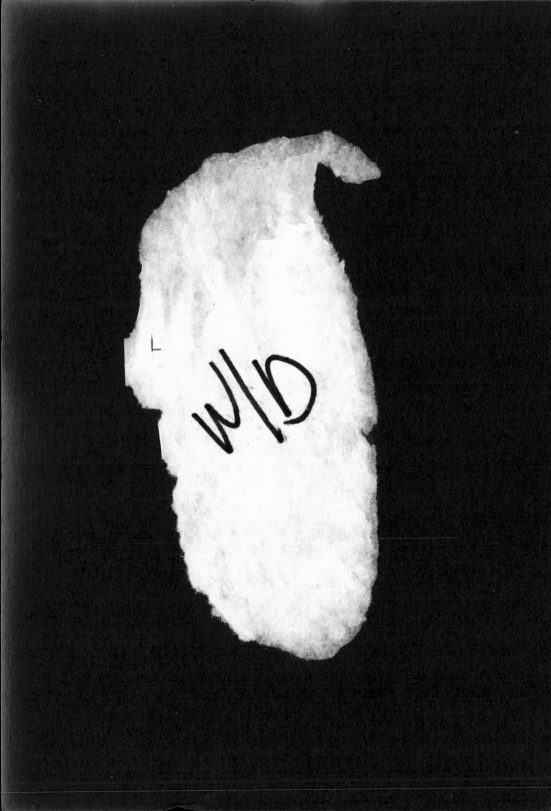